Welcome to the Octo[...]
Harlequin Presents!

This month read Sand[...] *The Sheikh's Defiant Bride*, the first book in her exciting trilogy THE SHEIKH TYCOONS. We also visit the Mediterranean, and two affluent heroes who aren't afraid to take what they want, in Julia James's *Greek Tycoon, Waitress Wife* and Robyn Donald's *His Majesty's Mistress*. Things begin to heat up at work (or should we say *after* work) for Abby in Anne Oliver's *Business in the Bedroom*. Maggie Cox also brings you a sexy office tale, this time involving an Italian tycoon and his unsuspecting personal assistant, in *Secretary Mistress, Convenient Wife*. Helen Bianchin weaves a story of attraction and convenience in *Purchased: His Perfect Wife,* in which cash-strapped Lara finds herself making a deal with her brooding stepbrother. Innocence is lost and passion abounds in *One Night with His Virgin Mistress* by Sara Craven, and housekeeper Liv's job description is more hands-on than most in *Housekeeper at His Beck and Call,* compliments of Susan Stephens.

We'd love to hear what you think about Harlequin Presents. E-mail us at Presents@hmb.co.uk, or join in the discussions at www.iheartpresents.com and www.sensationalromance.blogspot.com, where you'll also find more information about books and authors!

INNOCENT MISTRESS, VIRGIN BRIDE

Wedded and bedded for the very first time!

Classic romances from your favorite
Presents authors.

Available this month:

One Night with His Virgin Mistress
by Sara Craven

Available only from Harlequin Presents®.

Sara Craven

ONE NIGHT WITH HIS VIRGIN MISTRESS

INNOCENT MISTRESS, VIRGIN BRIDE

HARLEQUIN®

TORONTO • NEW YORK • LONDON
AMSTERDAM • PARIS • SYDNEY • HAMBURG
STOCKHOLM • ATHENS • TOKYO • MILAN • MADRID
PRAGUE • WARSAW • BUDAPEST • AUCKLAND

ISBN-13: 978-0-373-12765-8
ISBN-10:   0-373-12765-0

ONE NIGHT WITH HIS VIRGIN MISTRESS

First North American Publication 2008.

Copyright © 2008 by Sara Craven.

This edition published by arrangement with Harlequin Books S.A.

® and TM are trademarks of the publisher. Trademarks indicated with ® are registered in the United States Patent and Trademark Office, the Canadian Trade Marks Office and in other countries.

www.eHarlequin.com

Printed in U.S.A.

All about the author…
Sara Craven

SARA CRAVEN was born in South Devon,
England, and grew up surrounded by books
in a house by the sea. After leaving grammar
school she worked as a local journalist,
covering everything from flower shows to
murders. She started writing for Harlequin
in 1975. Sara Craven has appeared as a
contestant on the U.K. Channel Four game
show *Fifteen to One,* and in 1997 won the title
of Television Mastermind of Great Britain.

Sara shares her Somerset home with several
thousand books and an amazing video and
DVD collection.

When she's not writing, she likes to travel in
Europe, particularly in Greece and Italy. She
loves music, theater, cooking and eating in
good restaurants, but reading will always be her
greatest passion.

Since the birth of her twin grandchildren in
New York City, she has become a regular visitor
to the Big Apple.

PROLOGUE

HE'D had, he decided, more than enough. First, there'd been that
burning nightmare of a journey, wondering if each moment would
be their last, then the flight in the Hercules, and now this damned
farce of a press conference with its endless questions.

When all he really wanted was complete solitude, an opportunity to get out of clothes that stank and felt as if they were
crawling, and a torrent of hot water to rid him of the dirt and the
fear and make him human again. And God help anyone who got
in his way.

But now the idiot female reporter in the front row was batting
her eyelashes at him once more. She'd been behaving as if she
knew him, he thought wearily. And what was that all about?

'So,' she said, 'can you describe for my readers how you felt?'

'I was running for my life,' he said tersely. 'What do you think?'

'But you were the leader,' she went on. 'You got everyone to
safety. What's it like, finding you're a hero?'

'Madam,' he said curtly, 'I'm tired and filthy, and no one's
bloody hero. Not now. Not ever. I simply did my job. And, if
you've nothing more sensible to ask, I'm out of here.'

They'd laid on a car to take him home, and he was thankful,
knowing he wouldn't have been fit to drive himself. He was also
grateful that, by some miracle, he still had his wallet and his keys
and that soon he'd be able to find sanctuary and the peace he craved.

Yet as soon as he walked into the flat and closed the door behind him, his senses, honed by the dangers of the past few days and nights, told him that something was wrong. That he was not alone.

He stood, listening intently for a moment, recognising that it was the sound of a shower he could hear, then went soft-footed down the hallway towards his bedroom.

If *he's* still here, invading my space, he thought, I may well kill him.

He strode into the bathroom and halted, his furious gaze fixed incredulously on the slender shape clearly visible behind the glass walls of the shower cabinet.

'God in heaven,' he spat under his breath, 'I don't believe this.'

And he stepped forward and wrenched open the doors of the shower to reveal a naked, beautiful and terrified girl.

CHAPTER ONE

A week earlier

'IT SEEMS almost too good to be true,' Tallie Paget said with a sigh.

'In which case, it probably is,' her friend Lorna cautioned dourly. 'You hardly know this guy. For heaven's sake, take care.'

Tallie gave her a reassuring smile. 'But that's exactly what I shall be doing, don't you see? Taking care of Kit Benedict's flat while he's in Australia. Living rent-free, with just the electricity and heating bills to pick up, which I shall naturally be keeping to an absolute minimum.

'That has to be better than starving in a garret while I get the book finished—even if I found a garret I could afford.'

She paused. 'There's a word for this kind of thing.'

'I know there is,' said Lorna. 'Insanity.'

'Serendipity, actually,' Tallie informed her. 'Making happy and accidental discoveries, according to the dictionary. Just think—if I hadn't had an evening job in one of the wine bars which Kit's company supplies, and he hadn't seen me scouring the evening paper for a shed in someone's garden at less than a thousand pounds a month, none of this would have happened.'

'And moving out of your present flat,' Lorna asked dryly. 'Is that another happy accident?'

'No, of course not.' Tallie looked down at her empty coffee cup. 'But I can't stay there, not under the circumstances. You must see that. And Josie made it quite clear she wasn't planning to move out and live…with him.'

'God, she's a charmer, your cousin,' said Lorna. 'It wouldn't surprise me if she asked you to be her bridesmaid.'

'Nor me.' Tallie bit her lip. 'I can hear her now. "But Natalie, Mother will be *mortified* if you refuse. And it isn't as if you and Gareth were ever *really* involved."'

'No,' said Lorna. 'And just as well, under the circumstances.'

Tallie sighed. 'I know. And I also know I'll come to see that myself one day.' Her voice wobbled slightly. 'But not quite yet.'

Lorna gave her a searching look. 'And this Kit Benedict—promise me you're not falling for him on the rebound.'

'Heavens, no,' Tallie said, aghast. 'I've told you. He's off to Australia touring vineyards to learn more about the business. Besides, he's not my type in the slightest.'

Her type, she thought with a pang, was tall, with blond hair falling across his forehead, blue eyes and a lazy smile. Kit Benedict, on the other hand, was medium height, dark, and rather too full of himself.

'He needs a house-sitter,' she went on. 'I need somewhere to live. Done deal.'

'So what's it like, this place of his? The usual bachelor pad, overflowing with empty bottles and take-away cartons?'

'The total opposite,' Tallie assured her more cheerfully. 'It's on the top floor of this Edwardian block, with an utterly fabulous living room—wonderful squashy sofas and chairs, mixed in with genuine antiques, plus views all over London. There's a kitchen to die for, and two massive bedrooms. Kit said I could use whichever I wanted, so I'm having his—the master with its own gorgeous bathroom.'

Her room at Josie's was like a shoe box, she thought. One narrow single bed, with a zip-up plastic storage container underneath it for her limited wardrobe. No cupboard, so the rest of her clothes were hanging from two hooks on the back of the door. One tiny table, fortunately just large enough for her laptop, and a stool.

But then her cousin had never really wanted her there in the first place. Her offer of accommodation had been grudgingly made after family pressure, but neither she nor her flatmate Amanda, who occupied the two decent-sized bedrooms, had ever made Tallie feel welcome.

But the rent was cheap, so she'd have put up and shut up for as long as it took—if it hadn't been for Gareth.

Wincing inwardly, she hurried on. 'In fact, the whole flat is absolutely immaculate because there's a cleaner, Mrs Medland, who comes in twice a week. Kit says she's a dragon with a heart of gold, and I don't even have to pay for her. Apparently, some legal firm sees to all that. And I send the mail on to them too.'

She took a deep breath. 'And, from tomorrow, it will be all mine.'

'Hmm,' said Lorna. 'What I can't figure altogether is how it can possibly be all his—unless he actually owns this wine importing concern he works for.'

Tallie shook her head. 'Far from it. Apparently the flat is part of some family inheritance.' She paused. 'There's even a room that Kit uses as an office, and he says I can work in there and use the printer. I'm spoiled for space.'

Lorna sighed. 'Well, I suppose I have to accept that the whole situation's above board and you've actually fallen on your feet at last. I just wish you could have moved into Hallmount Road with us but, since Nina's boyfriend arrived, we're practically hanging from the light fittings as it is.'

'Honestly,' Tallie told her, 'everything's going to be fine.'

And I only wish I felt as upbeat as I sound, she thought as she walked back to the advertising agency where she'd been temping for the past three weeks, filling in for a secretary who'd been laid low by a vicious bout of chickenpox. She'd soon adapted to the strenuous pace of life at the agency, proving, as she'd done in her other placements, that she was conscientious, efficient and highly computer-literate. At the same time she'd revelled in the stimulation of its creative atmosphere.

In fact, it had been one of the nicest jobs she'd had all year and she was sorry it had come to an end, especially when her immediate boss had hinted that it could become a permanency. That she might even become a copywriter in due course.

And maybe Lorna was right and she was insane to throw away that level of security for a dream. On the other hand, she knew that she'd been given a heaven-sent opportunity to be a writer and if she didn't grasp it she might regret it for the rest of her life.

Everything she'd done that year had been with that aim in mind. All her earnings from the wine bar, and as much as she could spare from her daytime salary, had gone into a savings account to support her while she wrote. She'd be living at subsistence level, but she was prepared for that.

And all because she'd entered a competition in a magazine to find new young writers under the age of twenty-five. Entrants had been required to produce the first ten thousand words of a novel and Tallie, eighteen years old and bored as she'd waited for her A level exam results, had embarked on a story about a spirited girl who'd disguised herself as a man and undertaken a dangerous, adventure-strewn odyssey across Europe to find the young army captain she loved and who was fighting in Wellington's Peninsular Army.

She hadn't won, or even been placed, but one of the judges was a literary agent who'd contacted her afterwards and asked her to lunch in London.

Tallie had accepted the invitation with slight trepidation, but Alice Morgan had turned out to be a brisk middle-aged woman with children of her own who'd been through the school and university system, and who seemed to understand why career choices were not always cut and dried.

'My brother Guy always knew he wanted to be a vet like Dad,' Tallie had confided over the wonders of sea bass followed by strawberry meringue at the most expensive restaurant she'd ever visited. 'And at school they think I should go on to university and read English or History, before training as a teacher. But I'm really not sure, especially when I'll have a student loan to pay off once I qualify. So I'm taking a gap year while I decide.'

'Have you never considered writing as a career?'

Tallie flushed a little. 'Oh, yes, for as long as I can remember, but at some time in the future. I always thought I'd have to get an ordinary job first.'

'And this gap year—how will you spend that?'

Tallie reflected. 'Well, Dad always needs help in the practice. And I've done a fairly intensive computer course, so I could find office work locally.'

Mrs Morgan leaned back in her chair. 'And what happens to Mariana, now in the hands of smugglers? Does she get consigned to a file marked "might have been"? Or are you going to finish her story?'

'I hadn't really thought about it,' Tallie confessed. 'To be honest, I only wrote that first bit for fun.'

'And it shows.' Alice Morgan smiled at her. 'It's not perfect, but it's a good rip-roaring adventure told with real exuberance by a fresh young voice, and from the female angle. If you can sustain the storyline and the excitement at the same level, I think I could find more than one publisher who might be interested.'

'Goodness,' Tallie said blankly. 'In that case, maybe I should give it some serious thought.'

'That's what I like to hear,' the older woman told her cheerfully. 'One aspect you might consider is your hero, the dashing William. Is he based on anyone in particular—a boyfriend, perhaps?'

Tallie flushed. 'Oh, no,' she denied hurriedly. 'Nothing like that. Just—someone I see around the village sometimes. His parents have a cottage they use at weekends, but I…I hardly know him at all.'

Although I know his name—Gareth Hampton.

Mrs Morgan nodded. 'I rather got that impression because, as a hero, I couldn't get a handle on him either. And if Mariana is going to risk so much for love of him, you must make him worth the trouble. And there are one or two other things…'

Tallie caught the train home two hours later in something of a daze, the back of her diary filled with notes about those 'other things', but by the end of the journey any indecision about the immediate future was over and she had A Plan.

Her parents were astounded and a little dubious when she outlined it.

'But why can't you write at home?' her mother queried.

Because I'd never get anything done, thought Tallie with rueful affection. Between helping Dad when one of his assistants is sick, walking the dogs, giving a hand in the house and getting stuck into loads of batch baking for the WI or some do at the village hall, I'd always be on call for something.

She said, 'Mrs Morgan emphasised that I need to get my research right, and living in the city is just so convenient for that. I'm going to spend my Christmas and birthday money on a subscription to the London Library. Then I'll do what Lorna's done and find a flat-share with two or three other girls. Live as cheaply as I can.'

Mrs Paget said nothing, but pursed her lips, and a few days later she announced she'd been talking to Uncle Freddie and he'd agreed that living with strangers was unthinkable, and insisted that Tallie move in with her cousin Josie.

'He says her flat has a spare room, and she'll be able to help you find your feet in London,' she added.

Tallie groaned. 'Push me off the Embankment more likely. Mum, Josie's three years older than me and we haven't a thought in common. Besides, she and Aunt Val have always looked on us as the poor relations, you know that.'

'Well, I suppose we are in material terms,' said her mother. 'But not in any other way. Anyway,' she continued with cheerful optimism, 'I expect working for a living has smoothed off some of Josie's edges.'

Not so you'd notice, Tallie thought now as she rode up in the lift to the agency floor. At least, not where I'm concerned. And waiting on tables in the evening as well as holding down a day job may have been tough, but at least it's kept me out of the flat and away from her.

And, more recently, by dint of working until closing time and beyond at the wine bar, and leaving very early each morning, buying coffee and a croissant en route to work, she'd managed to remain in comparative ignorance about whether or not Gareth was now spending all his nights in Josie's room. Although the nagging pain deep within her told her the probable truth.

Stupid—stupid, she berated herself, to have built so much on a few lunches and a couple of weekend walks. But Gareth had been her 'bright particular star' for almost as long as she could remember, and simply spending time with him had seemed like a promise of paradise.

Until the moment when she'd had to stand there numbly, watching her star go out and paradise disappear, she thought bracing herself against the inevitable pain.

However, it was her last day as a member of the employed, and she wasn't going to break her self-imposed rule of never taking her personal problems into the workplace. So she straightened her shoulders, nailed on a smile and marched through the double glass doors into the open plan office beyond.

In the event, it turned out to be a much shorter afternoon than she'd expected. Before it was half over, her boss called the other staff together, champagne was produced and the managing director made a brief speech about what a valuable team member she'd been and how much she'd be missed.

'And if the next job doesn't work out as planned, we're only a phone call away,' he added, and Tallie heard a wobble in her voice as she thanked him.

When she called at the temps bureau later to collect her money, the manageress there also made it clear she was loath to lose her services.

'You've always been so reliable, Natalie,' she mourned. 'Isn't there a number where I can reach you in case of emergency?'

'I'm afraid not,' Tallie said firmly. Apart from her family and Lorna, no one was having the contact number at Albion House. Kit had made it clear she was not to hand it out to all and sundry, and she was happy to go along with that.

Besides, she was going to need every ounce of concentration she possessed for her book, which completely ruled out being at

the beck and call of The Relief Force, as the bureau titled itself.
They would just have to manage without her, she thought, although
she had to admit it was nice to be needed, if only in a work sense.

Meanwhile, finishing early today meant she would have the flat
to herself when she got back, and she could do her packing before
she set off for her final stint at the wine bar. So many doors closing,
she thought, but another massive one about to open in front of her,
and who knew what might lie beyond it.

At the flat, she made herself some coffee from what little was
left in the jar. In theory, they all bought their own groceries. In
practice, Josie and Amanda were always too busy for a regular
supermarket shop, and they used whatever was available.

The prospect of living on her own for the first time was fairly
daunting, but at least there would be fewer minor irritations to cope
with, Tallie told herself as she unzipped the storage box. She didn't
have many clothes—just the plain black skirts she wore for work
with an assortment of blouses and a grey checked jacket, the three
pairs of jeans that constituted leisurewear, a few T-shirts, a couple
of sweaters and a handful of cheap and cheerful chain store undies.

And right at the bottom of the box, neatly folded, was the shirt.
Almost, but not quite, forgotten. Slowly, she took it out, letting
the ivory silk slide through her hands, watching the shimmer of
the mother-of- pearl buttons. Allowing herself the pain of this one
last memory.

She'd been working for a firm of City accountants, she recalled,
and had been sent to fetch a tray of coffee for a clients' meeting from
the machine in the reception area. As she'd been on her way back,
going past the lift, the doors had opened and someone had emerged
in a hurry, cannoning into her and spilling the coffee everywhere.

'Oh, God.' A man's voice, appalled. 'Are you all right—not
scalded?'

'The drinks are never hot enough for that.' But there was a
hideous mess on the carpet and her once-crisp white shirt was
splashed and stained across the front and down one sleeve, plus
damp patches on her skirt too, she realised ruefully.

She knelt swiftly, reaching for the scattered paper cups. Aware, as she did so, that her assailant had also gone down on one knee to help her, but that he'd paused and was staring at her rather than the job in hand.

Looking up in turn, she recognised him instantly, her lips parting in a shocked gasp. 'Gareth,' she said unsteadily. 'I mean—Mr Hampton.'

'Gareth will do.' His sudden smile dazzled her like the sun breaking through clouds. 'And you're Guy Paget's little sister. What on earth are you doing here, miles from Cranscombe? Apart from being drowned in coffee, that is?'

'I live in London now,' she said quickly. 'Mr Groves's assistant is on holiday. I'm the temp. Or the ex-temp unless I get this mess cleared up quickly,' she added, seeing Mr Groves himself approaching, his face a mask of disapproval.

'All my fault, I'm afraid.' Gareth rose to meet him, spreading his hands in charming apology. 'I wasn't looking where I was going and nearly knocked poor little Natalie for six.'

'Oh, please don't concern yourself, my dear boy.' The look he sent Tallie was rather less gracious. 'Bring another tray to the conference room, Miss Paget, then call maintenance. This carpet will need to be properly cleaned. And tidy yourself too, please.'

The last instruction proved the most difficult to follow. Tallie did her best in the cloakroom with a handful of damp tissues but felt she'd only made matters worse. And the most sickening thing of all was the knowledge that Susie Johnson was in the meeting in her place, taking notes and feasting her eyes on Gareth at the same time.

I had no idea he was a client, she thought wistfully, wishing that she'd put on eye make-up that morning and was now wearing something other than a coffee-stained rag. Something that would have made him see her as rather more than Guy's kid sister.

Yet that was hardly likely, she acknowledged with a soundless sigh, remembering some of the girls he'd brought down to the cottage over the years. Slender creatures with endless legs, designer tans and artfully tousled hair.

Tallie's hair was the same light mouse-brown she'd been born with and it hung, straight as rainwater, to her shoulders. And while her mother loyally told her she had 'a pretty figure', she knew she was an unfashionable version of thin. Her creamy skin and hazel eyes, with their fringe of long lashes, were probably her best features, she thought judiciously, but her nose and mouth hadn't come out of any box marked 'Alpha Female'.

In a way, it was astonishing that Gareth should have remembered her at all, particularly as natural shyness combined with inexplicable adolescent yearnings had invariably made her vanish into any convenient doorway at his approach. She wasn't aware that he'd ever favoured her with a first glance, let alone a second.

And she'd now blown any chance she had of appearing cool, composed and efficient. A pillar of young serenity in the staid adult world of accountancy.

'Oh, Miss Paget's wonderful,' she imagined Mr Groves saying. 'I don't know how we ever managed without her.'

And pigs might take flight, she told herself, turning away from the mirror with another sigh.

But if she'd hoped to catch another glimpse of Gareth, she was to be disappointed. Instead, she was immediately waylaid by Mrs Watson, the office manager, who looked her over, compressed her lips and sent her off to the cubby-hole where the photocopier was housed with a pile of paperwork to be replicated.

And, by the time she emerged, Gareth was long gone and Susie Johnson was smiling smugly and reporting that he hadn't been able to take his eyes off her legs during the meeting.

She was about to leave for her coffee and sandwich lunch, buttoning her jacket to conceal the worst of her stained shirt, when Sylvia, the receptionist, called her over. 'This was delivered for you a few minutes ago.'

'This' was a flat package wrapped in violet and gold paper. And, inside, enclosed in tissue, was a silk shirt—soft, fragile and quite the most expensive garment she'd ever had the chance to own.

The accompanying card said:

To make amends for the one I ruined. I'll be waiting to hear if it's the right size from one o'clock onwards in the Caffe Rosso. G.

As she fastened the small buttons, the silk seemed to shiver against her warm body, clinging to her slender curves as if it loved them. A perfect fit, she thought. As if it was some kind of omen.

Against the ivory tone, her skin looked almost translucent and even her hair had acquired an added sheen. While her eyes were enormous—luminous with astonished pleasure.

Lunch, she thought with disbelief. I'm having lunch with Gareth Hampton, which is almost—a date. Isn't it?

Well, the answer to that was—no, as she now knew. As it had been brought home to her with a stinging emphasis that had almost flayed the flesh from her bones.

Like the false bride in the fairy tale, she thought, who'd put on a wedding dress that didn't belong to her and been destroyed as a result.

And kneeling there in her tiny room with that lovely, betraying thing in her hands, she shivered.

She folded it over and over again, her hands almost feverish, until it was reduced to a tiny ball of fabric, then wrapped it tightly in a sheet from a discarded newspaper and buried it deep in the kitchen bin on her way out to the wine bar.

Wishing, as she did so, that her emotions could be so easily dealt with—could be rolled up and discarded without a trace. Only it didn't work like that, and she would have to wait patiently until the healing process was over—however long it might take.

It will be better, she told herself fiercely, when I'm away from here. Everything is going to be better. It—has to be…

And when, the following evening, she found herself in sole occupation of her new domain, her belongings unpacked and her laptop set up in the study, she began to feel her new-found optimism could be justified.

It hadn't all been plain sailing. There'd been a final confrontation with her cousin that she'd have preferred to avoid.

'Quite apart from the inconvenience of having to find someone else for your room, do you realise the stick I'm going to get from Dad when he finds you've moved out?' Josie demanded shrilly. 'And that I don't even know where you've gone?'

Tallie shrugged. 'You're not my babysitter,' she countered. 'Besides, I thought you'd be glad to see the back of me.'

'Oh, for God's sake.' Josie glared at her. 'You're not still obsessing about Gareth, surely? Isn't it time you started to grow up?'

'More than time,' Tallie returned crisply. 'Consider this the first step.'

As a consequence, she'd arrived at Albion House, bag and baggage, much earlier than arranged, only to find Kit Benedict clearly impatient to be off, as if she'd kept him waiting.

'Now, you do remember everything I've told you?' he said, hovering. 'The fuse-box, the alarm system, and how to work the television. And you won't forget to forward any post to Grayston and Windsor? That's pretty vital.'

'Of course,' she said. She smiled at him, trying to look confident. 'I am fairly efficient, you know. I could have supplied references.'

'Well, I didn't really have time for that. Besides, Andy at the wine bar reckoned you were all right, and he's a shrewd judge.' He paused. 'My friends all know I'm going to be away, so you shouldn't have to fend off many phone calls. But if anyone should ring, just say Mr Benedict is away for an indefinite period.' He paused. 'And if they ask, save yourself a lot of hassle and tell them you're the cleaner.'

Why not the truth? Tallie wondered, but decided it was not worth pursuing as the problem was unlikely to arise.

'There's stuff in the fridge to finish up,' he added over his shoulder as he headed into the hall where his designer luggage was stacked. 'Clean bedding in both the rooms, and the laundry calls each Wednesday. Also, move whatever you need to out of the closets and drawers to make room for your things. Any emergencies, talk to the lawyers. They'll sort everything out.'

And he departed in a waft of the rather heavy aftershave he affected, leaving Tallie staring after him in vague unease. What emergencies did he have in mind? she asked herself wryly. Fire, flood, bubonic plague?

Although he was probably just trying to cover all eventualities, assure her there was back-up in place if necessary, she thought as she began to look round in earnest. Starting with the kitchen.

The 'stuff in the fridge' he'd mentioned was already finished and then some, she thought, eyeing it with disfavour. There were a few wizened tomatoes, some eggs well past their sell-by date, a hard piece of cheese busily developing its own penicillin and a salad drawer that made her stomach squirm.

Cleaning out the refrigerator and then restocking it at the nearest supermarket would be her first priority.

And her next, lying down on one of those enormous sofas and relaxing completely. Listening to the peace of this lovely place and letting herself soak up its ambience.

It was, she thought with faint bewilderment, the last kind of environment she'd have expected Kit Benedict to inhabit. Where he was concerned, the contents of the fridge seemed to make far more sense than the elegant furniture and Persian rugs.

It was a background that would have suited Gareth perfectly, she mused, her face suddenly wistful, imagining him lounging on the opposite sofa, glass of wine in hand, his hair gleaming against the dark cushions. Smiling at her…

Stop torturing yourself, she ordered silently. There's no future in that kind of thinking and you know it.

She managed to distance any other might-have-beens by keeping determinedly busy for the rest of the day. Settling herself in so that the real work could start in the morning. And the blues remained at bay during the evening, thanks to the plasma screen television that only appeared when a button was pressed in a section of panelling, but seemed to have every channel known to the mind of man available at a flourish of the remote control.

How entirely different from the TV set at the other flat, which seemed permanently stuck on BBC One, she thought. Although not everything had changed for the better, of course. The news still seemed uniformly depressing, with no sign of peace in the Middle East, another rise in the price of petrol, which would cost her father dear with all the miles he had to travel to visit sick animals, and a breaking story about an attempted military coup in some remote African state.

Sighing, Tallie restored the screen to its hiding place and went to bed.

And what a bed, she thought, stretching luxuriously. Quite the biggest she'd ever occupied, with the most heavenly mattress and pure linen sheets and pillowcases. And great piles of towels in the bathroom too, and a snowy bathrobe hanging on the back of the door.

She was almost asleep when the phone rang. She rolled across the bed, reaching blearily for the receiver. The caller started speaking at once, a woman's voice, low-pitched and husky, saying a man's name, then, in a swift rush of words, 'Darling, you're there—what a relief. I've been so worried. Are you all right?'

Tallie swallowed, remembering Kit's suggested formula. 'I'm sorry,' she said politely. 'Mr Benedict is away for an indefinite period.'

She heard a sharp intake of breath at the other end and the voice changed—became clipped, imperious. 'And who precisely are you, may I ask?'

There was no point in saying she was the cleaner—not at this ridiculous time of night, thought Tallie. Besides, that rather hectoring tone—the phrasing of the question—sounded just like Josie, and it riled her.

'Just a friend,' she said brightly and rang off.

She was half-expecting the caller to ring back, but the phone remained silent.

And just as she was drifting off again, it occurred to her that the name the unknown woman had said at the start of the conversation had not sounded like Kit at all, but something completely different.

I must be wrong, she told herself drowsily. After all, I was half asleep. Anyway, it's too late to worry about that now—much too late.

And, turning over with a sigh, she closed her eyes.

CHAPTER TWO

TALLIE closed down her laptop and leaned back in the padded black leather chair with a sigh that contained more relief than satisfaction.

At last, she thought. At last I seem to be back on track.

She could acknowledge now how scared she'd been, gambling on her future in this way, especially as she'd made comparatively little progress with her story since that momentous lunch with Mrs Morgan.

But then conditions over the past months had hardly been conducive, she reminded herself ruefully. Her free time had been severely limited and when she had tried to work at the flat she'd had to compete with the constant noise of Josie's television and Amanda's stereo system blasting through the thin panels of her door.

And then, of course, there'd been Gareth's intervention...

She took a deep breath, damming back the instinctive pang. Well, at least she now had an insight into what it was like to fall in love, even a little. Could see why a girl like Mariana might give up so much to pursue this reckless adventure if it meant she'd be reunited with a man she wanted so desperately.

Up to then, she realised, she hadn't given much thought to her story's emotional input, concentrating instead on the fun of it all— her heroine's rollicking escape from her stern guardian and the threat of an arranged marriage.

Now, she realised that Mariana's decision would have far more impact if she was, instead, deserting a loving home with parents who were simply over-protective, who knew the uncertainties of a soldier's life and wished to spare her danger and heartache.

And this would naturally change the entire emphasis of the book.

Less of a light-hearted romp, she told herself, however enjoyable that had been to invent, and more of a story about passionate love and its eventual reward, which, in itself, was going to present her with all kinds of problems.

Because the events of the last few weeks had brought home to her how signally—ridiculously—unacquainted she was with any form of passion. Or even likely to be.

She swallowed past the sudden tightness in her throat. Oh, well, she told herself with false brightness, she'd cross that bridge when she came to it. After all, imagination was a wonderful thing.

And it would help that she wouldn't have to write too much about 'doing it' until the very end of the book because, no matter how precarious the situations she found herself enduring, Mariana was obviously saving herself for marriage to her gorgeous William, with his smiling blue eyes and his slanting smile.

And the way he talked to her as if he was really interested in what she had to say…

She stopped hastily. Oh, God—this wasn't the book at all. She was back to Gareth again and the endless, punishing reliving of every precious moment she'd spent with him. All that witless, pitiful self-deception over it being the start of something important—even valuable—which had begun with that lunch at the Caffe Rosso.

She'd been tongue-tied at first, trying to express her halting thanks for the beautiful shirt.

'Well,' he said, 'it seemed the least I could do. Henry Groves is a terrific accountant, but appearances matter to him.' He grinned. 'I bet that carpet in reception has been shampooed already.'

It was quite an ordinary lunch—lasagne and a couple of glasses of the house red—but for Tallie it was caviare and champagne, nectar and ambrosia all rolled into one.

Gareth wanted to know what she was doing in London. 'I had you down as a home bird—sticking close to Cranscombe.'

In other words, as dull as ditchwater.

She looked down at her plate. 'I'm having a kind of gap year—while I decide what I want to do.' She decided not to mention the novel. It seemed pretentious to do so while it was still in such an embryonic stage. 'And how's the world of law?'

'It has its moments.' He paused. 'I'm probably going to specialise in tax. That seems a reasonably lucrative field.'

'You don't want to defend master criminals?'

'That always sounds more glamorous than it really is.' He shrugged. 'And, on the whole, they deserve what they get.' He signalled for the dessert menu. 'Did you know my parents are deserting Cranscombe too? They've sold the cottage and are buying a place in Portugal—warmer climate and masses of golf.'

'Oh.' She looked at him, startled. 'So if you hadn't come to the office today, I might never have seen you again.'

The moment she said it, she could have bitten out her tongue. Oh, God, she thought despairingly, she couldn't have given herself away more blatantly if she'd taken all her clothes off in front of him.

She felt the mortified colour rising in her face and wanted nothing more than to get up and run out of the restaurant. Only to find her hand taken, her fingers caressed very gently by his.

'Even worse,' he said, 'I might not have seen you either. Shall we celebrate our fortunate escape from disaster with some tiramisu?'

Over coffee, he suggested that they should meet again on Saturday evening—go to the cinema, perhaps, or a club, forcing Tallie to explain, her voice husky with disappointment, that she had an extra job, which she couldn't afford to lose.

Yet he didn't seem offended at all. He suggested instead that they meet for lunch on the river and afterwards go walking.

'The best way to see London is on foot,' he told her. 'And I can't wait to show it to you.'

In a way, she was almost relieved, because she'd seen Josie and Amanda dressed—or undressed—to go out to dinner, or clubbing, and knew that her current wardrobe simply couldn't cope. That becoming Gareth's girlfriend could take some living up to and she might even have to raid her precious savings account.

She floated back to the office on a cloud of euphoria, almost unable to believe that she was going to see him again. That he wanted to spend time with her. So lost in bliss, in fact, that it never occurred to her to question why this should be.

And Saturday afternoon passed like a dream. Gareth was extremely knowledgeable about the capital—knew all kinds of interesting places and fascinating stories, and she listened, rapt.

He told her about his job too, and the other barristers in his chambers, and about his own flat-share with a couple of university friends, waxing almost lyrical about how terrific Notting Hill was—great ambience, great restaurants.

It was clear that city living appealed to him far more than the country ever would. That he didn't regret the cottage at Cranscombe one bit, and this saddened her a little.

However, the only really awkward moment came when they were about to part and she realised he was going to kiss her, and she was so nervous—so unpractised—that it turned into little more than an embarrassing bumping of noses and chins.

She spent the whole evening mentally kicking herself at the memory. Telling herself that she should have kept still as he'd bent towards her, closed her eyes, smiling, as she raised her mouth to meet his. That he couldn't possibly know she'd only been kissed three or four times before, and generally because it had seemed rude to refuse.

And that Gareth's had been the first kiss that should have—would have—meant something.

Well, next time—and he'd arranged to see her on the following Saturday too—she would be prepared, and she would make sure that she was much less inept.

She spent the whole week in such a state of anticipation that reality was almost bound to be an anticlimax. Yet it started well—a glorious spring afternoon—and this time it wasn't so much of a guided tour because Gareth suggested that they went strolling in

Hyde Park. It seemed full of couples. They were everywhere Tallie looked—young, happy people, walking hand in hand, sitting close on benches—always looking at each other, always touching—even lying on the grass wrapped in each others' arms, oblivious to all but themselves.

And she found herself moving nearer to Gareth as they walked, longing for him to take her hand or put his arm round her. That she wanted to be part of a couple too—half of him, with all that it would mean. Something she'd never contemplated before—or even desired…

But a sideways glance told her this seemed unlikely. He was gazing into space, not at her, seemingly lost in thought, even frowning a little.

She tried to keep her voice light, to recapture the almost intimacy of the previous week. 'A penny for them.'

'What? Oh, I see.' He hesitated. 'I was thinking about something we could do. That maybe we might…'

Her heart almost stopped. What was he going to say—to suggest? That the Park was too public and they should go back to—his place? Oh, please, she thought. Please, let it be that. Because even if nothing happened, and she knew it was far too soon—that she should be ashamed of herself for even thinking that, it went against every principle she'd ever had—at least it would show that he was beginning to consider her as part of his life. That she mattered to him.

It would prove, if nothing else, that he wanted her to meet his friends, maybe drink some wine, and, later, go out for a meal, even if she wasn't strictly dressed for it. She tried to think of an excuse she could give Andy at the wine bar for not working that evening—the first time she would ever have let him down.

He went on, 'I was going to say that tea at Fortnums would be nice.'

'Yes,' she said. 'Lovely.' And tried not to feel disappointed. Reminded herself that it was still early days and the fact that he didn't want to rush her into anything was a good sign. A sign that he respected her. And a warning that she must let things develop at their own pace.

She was still thinking that as they walked up Piccadilly. As they reached Fortnums and paused at the door because someone was coming out.

'Natalie,' Josie said, 'I didn't know you could afford places like this.' She turned, self-assured and smiling, to look at Gareth. Tallie watched her eyes widen, her gaze become fixed. There was a pause— a count of a few heartbeats—then she said, 'And who's this?'

'Gareth Hampton. A—a friend from Cranscombe.'

'Goodness,' Josie said lightly. 'And to think I used to go out of my way to avoid the place.' She smiled. 'Well, friend from Cranscombe, I'm Natalie's cousin, Josephine Lester, and I bet she hasn't told you about me either.'

'No.' Gareth's voice sounded odd, almost hoarse. 'No, as a matter of fact, she didn't.' He was staring at her too, his face set, almost stunned.

Tallie had the oddest impression that the pair of them were locked into some kind of exclusion zone—surrounded by a barrier like a force field which she would never be able to penetrate. It was such a strong impression that she almost took a step backwards.

She heard herself say in a small wooden voice she barely recognised, 'We were going to have tea.'

Was aware that they'd both turned and looked at her in surprise, as if they'd forgotten her very existence. Then realised that was exactly what they'd done.

Josie was smiling again. She said softly, 'What a lovely idea.'

Somehow, Tallie found she was pushing up her sleeve, glancing at her watch. 'Only I didn't realise how late it's getting, and I'm due at work pretty soon.' It was still only mid-afternoon, but she knew numbly that she could have said she was off bungee-jumping from the dome of St Paul's without it registering with either of them. She shared a swift meaningless smile between them. 'So, I'll leave you to it. Enjoy your tea.'

She went off, walking fast enough to convey an impression of haste—someone who needed to be somewhere else—but not so fast it would look as if she was running away.

Especially when there was nowhere to run to.

If the flat had seemed cramped before, it quickly became a living nightmare. It seemed that, no matter what time of the day or night she ventured out of her room, Gareth was there, and it was a minor consolation to know that Amanda was no more pleased with the situation than herself, or that she and Josie were constantly bickering about it.

'No live-in boyfriends,' she heard Amanda say stormily. 'That was the rule we made, yet here he is.'

'But he doesn't live here,' Josie returned. She gave a little throaty giggle. 'He just—stays over sometimes.'

'Seven nights a week is hardly "sometimes",' Amanda said coldly, going into her room and slamming the door.

Tallie did her best to be unobtrusive, speaking politely if it was required, her face expressionless, determined not to reveal the bewildered heartache that tore into her each time she saw Gareth or heard his voice.

Once, and only once, she came back from work and found him there alone. She halted in palpable dismay, then, muttering, 'Excuse me,' made for her room.

But he followed. 'Look, Natalie, can we lighten up a bit?' he asked almost irritably. 'It's bad enough getting filthy looks from Amanda, without you creeping about as if I'd delivered some kind of death blow. And now Josie says you're moving out altogether.'

He added defensively, 'For God's sake, it's not as if there was ever—anything going on between us. You were Guy's little sister, that was all.'

Not for me—never for me…

She swung round to face him. 'And you were just being kind—giving a child a day or two out. A few treats. Was that it? I—I didn't realise.'

'Well, it could never have been anything more than that.'

'Why not?' She was suddenly past caring. 'Am I so totally repulsive?'

'No, of course not.' He spoke reluctantly, clearly sorry he'd ever begun the confrontation.

'Then what? Because I'd really like to know.'

He sighed. 'Are you sure about that?' He hesitated, clearly embarrassed, then plunged in. 'Look, Natalie—it was perfectly obvious you've never been to the end of the street, let alone round the block. And I couldn't deal with that. In fact, I didn't even want to.'

She didn't pretend to misunderstand. 'I thought men liked that—knowing they were the first.'

'Not me.' He shook his head. 'I still have the scars from my one and only time with a virgin. My God, I had to spend hours pleading, a good time was not had by all, and afterwards she expected me to be eternally grateful.'

She stood, stricken, remembering low-voiced, rather giggly conversations at school between more worldly-wise friends, admitting that 'it' had hurt 'like hell' the first time—that, all in all, it had been messy, uncomfortable and incredibly disappointing. And then, the next time—miraculously—had begun to improve.

But it wouldn't have been like that with us—with me. I know it…

The thought came, aching, into her mind, and was instantly dismissed. Because the truth was she didn't know anything of the sort. And, anyway, the important thing now was to walk away, not crawl.

She lifted her chin. 'Well, whoever she was and, believe me, I don't want to know, my sympathies are entirely with her.' And she sauntered into her room, closing the door behind her.

It was, she thought, the last time she'd ever spoken to him. And maybe much of the pain she still felt about him was not so concerned with his preference for Josie—no one, she told herself, could help falling in love, and what she'd witnessed might have been a genuine *coup de foudre*—but the cruelly dismissive way he'd spoken about her sexual ignorance, as if it was some kind of blight. That it was her own fault that she hadn't been putting it about since she'd reached the age of consent.

However, it was impossible to erase him from her mind altogether, because he was still the image of William, her fictional hero, and too deeply entrenched in her imagination to change. Except that William was kind, loyal and tender, and Mariana would have the happy ending she deserved.

Unlike me, she thought, and sighed swiftly.

But she couldn't feel too dispirited for long—not in this lovely room. She loved the entire flat, especially the kitchen, and the wonderful *en suite* bathroom with its aquamarine tiles, huge power shower and enormous tub. But the office had to be her favourite of all—a big room filled with light and completely fitted out with pale oak furniture.

It was completely uncluttered, with not a stray scrap of paper in sight. Well, not until she'd arrived, anyway, she thought, wrinkling her nose. It was slightly more lived-in now.

Nor could she relate the Kit Benedict she'd encountered to all this orderly professionalism. Frankly, it had never occurred to her that working in the wine trade would require him to set up this kind of dedicated workplace at home.

Unless, like herself, he moonlighted, she thought, which in turn would explain how he could afford the array of suits with designer labels, the expensive shirts and handmade shoes she'd found in the master bedroom's fitted closets as she'd tried to make space for her own few things.

But, whatever Kit did in this room, he kept strictly to himself because everything was securely locked up—the desk drawers, the cupboards, the filing cabinets and the bookcases, which seemed, she noted with surprise, to be devoted to mathematics and scientific topics.

Not that it matters to me, Tallie told herself firmly. Unless it's illegal and the Metropolitan Police suddenly arrive.

But that was an unlikely scenario and, in the meantime, she had the use of the desk and the printer, and she provided her own stationery so she had no need or wish to pry any further.

She got up, stretching, then collected together the completed pages slipping them into the waiting folder before wandering off to the kitchen to put together some pasta carbonara.

She ate, as usual, from a tray on her lap in the sitting room. There was a dining room across the passage, but she never used it as it was clearly designed for smart dinner parties, not solitary suppers, and she found it a little daunting.

There was a drama series she wanted to watch on television and, while she was waiting for it to start, she took her plate and fork into the kitchen and loaded them into the dishwasher along with the utensils she'd used.

When she got back with her coffee, she found the start of her programme had been slightly delayed by an extended newscast. The situation in the African state of Buleza had deteriorated swiftly over the past few days. The initial coup had been defeated but the rebels had regrouped and a full-scale civil war had broken out. All British nationals had been evacuated from the capital, but there'd been concern over a group of engineers constructing a bridge across the Ubilisi in the north of the country who'd been cut off by the fighting.

According to the excited tones of the reporter covering the story, the men had now been traced and air-lifted to safety across the border. From there, they would be flown home, and the Foreign Office had a number for concerned relatives to call.

For once a happy ending, Tallie thought as the signature tune for her programme began and she curled up in her corner of the sofa to enjoy it. And that's what we all need—more happy endings.

The last of the groceries safely put away, Tallie straightened, moving her shoulders wearily. Thank goodness that's over for a while, she thought.

Shopping was never her favourite pastime at the best of times, and this afternoon the supermarket had been busy and the bus hot and crowded, forcing her to stand with her two heavy bags. To make matters worse, the journey had been held up by a collision between a car and a van. No one had been injured, but both vehicles had been damaged, tempers had been frayed and the police called as a result, so she'd got off and walked the last half mile back to the flat.

It was a humid, overcast day, as if a storm was threatening, and she felt grimy and frazzled, her hair sticking to her scalp. She'd have a shower before she prepared the salad for her evening meal, she decided with a sigh of anticipation.

In the bedroom, she chose clean underwear and a fresh pair of cotton trousers with a green scoop-neck top and left them on the bed. She undressed in the bathroom, thrusting her discarded clothing into the laundry basket, then stepped into the shower. She shampooed her hair vigorously and turned the water pressure to full as she rinsed the lather away, before beginning to apply her rose-scented body wash to her skin, smoothing away the remaining weariness and lingering aggravation of the day, then letting the water stream over her, lifting her face, smiling, to its power.

Then suddenly—shockingly—she became aware that she was no longer alone. Glimpsed a dark shadow, tall and menacing, outside the steamy glass of the cabinet. Felt the gush of cooler air as the sliding doors of the shower were wrenched open and someone—a total stranger—was standing there, staring in at her. A lean pillar of a man, wearing a shirt and trousers in stained and scruffy khaki drill.

Tallie had a horrified impression of black tousled hair, an unshaven chin, hands clenched aggressively at his sides and dark brows snapping together in furious astonishment as ice-cold green eyes swept over her.

She shrank back instinctively into the corner, cowering there, her voice cracking as she tried to scream and failed. As her own hands rose in a futile attempt to cover her body—to conceal her nakedness from this…predator, who was turning the worst—the ultimate nightmare into harsh reality. As fear warred with shame under his gaze.

Where had he come from? Had he been hiding somewhere in the flat, biding his time—choosing his moment? Her mind ran crazily like a rat trapped in a maze. Yet the door had been locked

*when she'd returned from shopping, and she'd re-locked it behind
her. It was the most basic security precaution, and never neglected,
so how could he have got in?*

'Turn that bloody water off.' He spoke above its rush, his voice
low-pitched and well-modulated, but grim as an Arctic wind. 'Then,
sweetheart, you have precisely one minute to explain who you are
and what the hell you're doing in my flat before I call the police.'

Ridiculously, the word 'police' brought a kind of fleeting reassur-
ance. It wasn't the kind of threat a rapist or a psychopath would use—
was it? she thought desperately, her fingers all thumbs as she forced
herself to deal with the shower flow, shivering with panic and burning
with embarrassment at the same time. And he'd said 'my flat', so what
was going on—apart from her own imminent death through shame?

'I'm waiting.' He took a towel from the rail and threw it towards
her and she snatched at it, huddling it almost gratefully round her
body as she struggled to make her voice work.

'I'm looking after the flat while Mr Benedict is away.' It was
hardly more than a shaken gasp.

'Is that a fact?' He looked her over again, standing with his
hands on his hips, the firm lips twisting. 'Well, now Mr Benedict
is back and I made no such arrangement, so I suggest you think
up another story fast.'

'No, you don't understand.' She put up a hand to push the
sodden tangle of hair back from her face and the towel slipped.
She grabbed at it, blushing. 'My agreement's with Kit Benedict—
who's in Australia. Are—are you a member of his family?'

'I'm the head of the damned family,' he returned icily. 'Kit, unfortunately, is my half-brother, and you, presumably, are one of
his little jokes—or compensation for some misdemeanour I have
yet to discover. Payment in kind rather than cash. My welcome
home present.'

The green eyes narrowed, their expression becoming less
hostile and more contemplative, bordering on amusement, and
Tallie felt fresh stirrings of panic under his renewed scrutiny.

'Under normal circumstances, of course, I wouldn't touch Kit's leavings,' he went on, as if he was thinking aloud. 'But there's been nothing normal about the past few eternally bloody days, and maybe finding a naked, pretty girl in my shower is immaculate timing. A hint that a few hours of mindless enjoyment could be just what I most need.' He began to unbutton his shirt. 'So put the water on again, darling, and I'll join you.'

'Keep away from me.' Tallie pressed herself against the tiled wall as if she was trying to disappear through it. Her voice was hoarse and trembling. 'I'm not anyone's leavings, least of all your brother's. We had—we have a business agreement, that's all.'

'Fine.' He dropped his shirt to the floor and started to unzip his trousers. He slanted a smile at her. 'And now your business is with me, only the terms have changed a little.'

'You don't understand,' she insisted more fiercely. 'I'm just here as the caretaker. Nothing more.'

'Then take care of me,' he said equably. 'You can start by washing my back.'

'No,' she said, 'I won't.' She swallowed. 'And I warn you now that if you come near me—if you dare try and lay a hand on me, I'll have you charged with rape. I swear it.'

There was a taut silence, then he said softly, 'You actually sound as if you mean that.'

'I do.' She lifted her chin. 'And you'd better also believe that I'm not involved with Kit and I never was, and never would be either. I think, in his own way, he's almost as obnoxious as you are.'

'Thank you.' There was an odd note in his voice.

'I came here simply to do a job and, until a few minutes ago, I didn't know you even existed. I thought this was his flat.'

'I'm sure it pleased him to give that impression.' He shrugged a bare shoulder, setting off a ripple of muscle that she would have preferred not to see. 'It always has. But let me assure you that the flat is mine and so is everything in it, including that inadequate towel you're clutching, and the bed where you've apparently been sleeping,' he added silkily, watching the colour storm back into her face at the implication of his words.

'In reality, I'm Kit's occasional and very reluctant host. And currently, for some reason which I'm sure you're eager to share with me, I seem to be yours too.'

She made a desperate stab at dignity. 'Naturally, I do see that you're…owed an explanation.'

'Perhaps we should postpone any discussion on the extent of your indebtedness for a more convenient moment.'

His soft-voiced intervention had her biting her lip, but she pressed on doggedly, 'However, my reasons for being here are perfectly genuine. I—I have nothing to hide.'

'No?' he queried, the green eyes measuring her with dancing cynicism. 'You could have fooled me.'

He strode over to the door and took down the bathrobe that hung there. 'And now I intend to take my shower whether you remain there or not,' he said as he returned. 'So I suggest you put this on and make yourself scarce—if your maidenly reluctance to pleasure me is actually genuine.'

He paused, holding the robe. 'Is it—or could you still be persuaded to offer a weary traveller the comfort of that charming body?'

'No,' she said, teeth gritted, 'I could not.'

He shrugged again, tossing the bundle of towelling into her arms. 'Then go. However, I should warn you that I'm still considering having you charged with trespass.' He observed her lips parting in a silent gasp of alarm and went on, 'But some good coffee—black, hot and strong—might help your cause.'

'Is that an order?' She tried a defiant note.

'Merely a suggestion,' he said. 'Which you'd do well to heed.'

He watched with open amusement as Tallie turned her back to manoeuvre herself awkwardly out of the wet towel and into the robe.

'Your modesty is delightful, if a little belated,' he commented dryly as she sidled out of the shower cabinet, looking anywhere but at him, the robe thankfully drowning her from throat to ankle. 'I'll join you and the coffee presently.'

He paused. 'And don't even think of doing a runner, because I would not find that amusing.'

'You mean before you've counted the spoons?' She glared at him.

'Before any number of things.' He stripped off the khaki trousers and kicked them away. 'I suggest the sitting room as suitably neutral territory. Unless you have a more interesting idea?' he added, his hands going to the waistband of his shorts. 'No? Somehow I thought not.'

And, as he casually dropped his final covering and walked into the shower, Tallie turned and fled, hearing, to her chagrin, his shout of laughter following her.

CHAPTER THREE

DON'T even think of doing a runner...

If only I could, Tallie thought bitterly as she switched on the percolator and set a cup, a saucer, cream jug and sugar bowl on a tray. I'd be out of here so fast, my feet wouldn't touch the ground.

But, unfortunately, it wasn't as simple as that. For one thing, she had nowhere else to go. For another, nearly everything she owned was in the master bedroom—and so, now, was the master. In her haste to get away from him, she'd even left her change of clothing strewn across the bed. His bed, she reminded herself, groaning inwardly.

She'd steeled herself to creep back at one point to retrieve it, but the bathroom door had been wide open, the sound of the shower only too audible, and she dared not risk being seen—or seeing him again either, she thought shuddering, so it had seemed more sensible to turn away.

Which meant that when she did have to face him in a short while, she'd still be swamped in yards of towelling that also didn't belong to her. But at least she'd be covered this time, she thought, a wave of heat sweeping over her as she remembered that remorseless green-eyed gaze assessing every detail of her quivering body.

Not to mention the way he'd casually stripped in front of her, which had almost been more of an insult...

Tallie swallowed. People reckoned that there came a time when you could look back at moments of truly hideous embarrassment and laugh about them, but she couldn't imagine any moment, however far into the future, when she would be able to find the events of the last half hour even remotely amusing. When remembering them would not make her want to curl up and die of shame.

She was already cringing at the prospect of her next confrontation with him. It had already occurred to her that her agreement with Kit Benedict had been purely verbal, and that she hadn't a scrap of paper to back up her claim that she was flat-sitting on his behalf.

That the real owner, however vile, probably had every right to regard her presence as trespass. But not to assume she was involved in some sordid relationship with his brother, she told herself hotly. A discarded plaything that could be…handed on for his own use. Or who might even be willing for that to happen.

If she was being honest, she had to admit she'd had a lucky escape. That if he'd decided her protests were simply coy and not to be taken seriously, then her nightmare could have taken on a whole new dimension that she didn't want to contemplate. His hands—touching her. That mocking mouth…

Shivering, she hurriedly refocused her train of thought.

Too good to be true…

Her own words came back to haunt her. Well, she knew the truth of that now. Realised how stupid she'd been to ignore the obvious pitfalls in such a casual arrangement. To dismiss the clear anomalies between the Kit Benedict she'd met and this serene, luxurious background he'd apparently appropriated as his own.

He'd never really belonged here, she thought. And she'd always suspected as much. But then, for God's sake, neither did Real Owner—the sexist thug with his scruffy hair, filthy clothes and three-day growth. He was even more out of place—like the brutal invader of a peaceful foreign territory. Inexperienced as she was, she'd sensed the danger in him, the anger like a coiled spring threatening to erupt.

Shivering, she wandered restively out into the passage, noting that the door to the master bedroom was now firmly shut. There was no sound from beyond it, or anywhere else, but the stillness and quiet she'd cherished suddenly seemed to have turned into an oppressive silence beating down on her. As if she was waiting for some other dreadful thing to happen.

Don't think like that, she advised herself, swallowing, as she retreated to the kitchen. Put those ghastly minutes in the bathroom behind you and try to behave normally. Moving in here was obviously a mistake, but you're not a criminal and he must see that.

She set the coffee pot on the tray and carried it through to the sitting room, placing it on a charming walnut table in front of one of the sofas.

Television, she thought. Men liked television. The first thing her father and Guy seemed to do when they walked into the house was switch on the set in the living room, whether or not there was anything they wanted to watch. Real Owner might well think along similar lines.

She clicked on to one of the major channels and stood for a moment, adjusting the sound. The picture on the screen was coming from an airfield, showing a plane coming in to land, and a group of weary, dishevelled men disembarking from it. About to turn away, Tallie sent them a casual glance, then paused, her eyes widening as she realised that the tall figure leading the ramshackle party down the plane steps looked horribly familiar.

No, she thought, transfixed in spite of herself. No, surely not.

'Glad to be safely home are the British engineers, who found themselves stranded by the civil war in Buleza,' said an authoritative voice-over. 'At the press conference following their arrival, Mark Benedict, the chief consultant on the Ubilisi bridge project, said it had been a major target for the opposition forces and, as a result, completely destroyed.'

Mark Benedict, she thought with a swift intake of breath. *Mark Benedict...* Then it really was him. It had to be.

She heard a step behind her and turned. 'My God,' she said huskily. 'You were out there—in that African country where there's been all the terrible fighting.'

'Yes,' he said. 'And, believe me, I don't need any reminders.' He took the remote control from her hand and the screen went blank.

He was hardly recognisable, Tallie thought blankly, apart, of course, from those amazing eyes. He certainly hadn't the kind of looks she admired but, now that he was clean-shaven, she had to admit that he had a striking face, with high cheekbones, a strong beak of a nose and a chin that was firm to the point of arrogance.

Altogether, there was a toughness about him that Kit signally lacked, she decided without admiration, something emphasised by the line of an old scar along one cheekbone and the evidence of a more recent injury at the corner of his mouth, accentuating the cynical twist which was probably habitual with him.

The over-long dark hair had been combed into some kind of damp, curling order and the lean, tawny body was, thankfully, respectably clad in chinos and a black polo shirt.

He looked at the coffee tray. 'Firstly,' he said, 'you can take away the cream and sugar, because I never use them, and, at the same time, bring me a mug in place of the after-dinner china. And, while you're there, bring another for yourself.'

'Is that really necessary?' Tallie lifted her chin. 'After all, it's hardly a social occasion.'

'A fair amount of business can also be settled over coffee.' His tone was quiet but brooked no arguments. 'So why not just do as I ask, Miss—er…'

'Paget,' she supplied curtly. 'Natalie Paget.'

'And I'm Mark Benedict, as I expect you already know.' He paused. 'Please don't look so stricken, Miss Paget. I assure you that you're just as unpleasant a shock to me as I am to you. So let's sit down with our coffee in a civilised manner and discuss the situation.'

'Civilised,' Tallie brooded as she trailed back to the kitchen with the unwanted items, was not a word she would ever apply to her unwanted host. But 'discuss' was hopeful, because it didn't suggest that he was planning to bring charges immediately.

However, knowing that all she was wearing was his bathrobe still placed her at a serious disadvantage, no matter how businesslike the discussion. As he was probably well aware, she told herself bitterly.

On her return to the sitting room, she accepted the mug that he filled and handed to her and sat down on the sofa opposite, hiding her bare feet under the folds of the robe—a nervous movement that she knew was not lost on him.

'So,' he began, without further preliminaries, 'you say Kit's in Australia. When did that happen and why?'

She looked down at her coffee. 'He went at the end of last week,' she returned woodenly. 'I understand it's a business trip—visiting various vineyards on behalf of the company he works for.'

The hard mouth relaxed into genuine amusement. 'Well, well,' he said softly, 'I bet Veronica didn't consider that was an option when she wangled the job for her baby boy.' He paused. 'He didn't ask you to go with him?'

'Of course not.' Tallie stiffened indignantly. 'I hardly know him.'

'That's not always a consideration,' he murmured. 'And, where Kit's concerned, it could be a positive advantage.' He leaned back against the cushions, apparently relaxed, but Tallie wasn't fooled. She could feel the tension quivering in the air, like over-stretched wire. 'Anyway, if it was such a brief acquaintance, how did you get to find out about this place?'

'It was his own suggestion,' she said defensively. 'He knew I was looking for somewhere cheap to live for a few months.'

His brows lifted. 'You regard this as some kind of doss-house?' he asked coldly.

'No—on the contrary—truly.' Tallie flushed hotly. 'I suppose when I came here and saw what it was like, I should have realised there was something…not right about the arrangement. But I was desperate, and grateful enough not to ask too many questions. And, anyway, I thought I could repay him by being the world's greatest flat-sitter. Looking after it as if it was my own.' She swallowed. 'Even better than my own.'

'Or, knowing he was going away, you could have decided to squat here.' His eyes were hard.

'No, I swear I didn't.' She met his gaze bravely. 'If you don't believe me, ask my former boss at the wine bar. He was there when your brother made the offer.' She took a gulp of the hot coffee to hearten her. 'Besides, a squatter wouldn't know about forwarding the mail to the lawyers, or have a key, or been told the security code—any of it.'

'You've been working in a wine bar?' He frowned slightly.

'Why not?' she challenged. 'It's a perfectly respectable occupation.'

'Respectable—sure.' He studied her curiously. 'But as a career? I'd have thought you'd want better than that.'

'Well,' she said tautly, 'as we're total strangers, that's hardly for you to judge.' She paused, then added reluctantly, 'Besides, I also had a day job working as a secretary for a temps agency. The bar was…extra.'

'I notice you keep using the past tense,' Mark Benedict commented. 'Am I to take it that you're no longer gainfully employed?'

'I'm no longer wage-earning,' she admitted. 'But I am working.'

'At what? Your questionable duties as flat-sitter won't take up too many hours in the day.'

She bit her lip, unwilling to expose her precious plan to his undoubted ridicule. She said primly, 'I'm engaged on…on a private project.'

'As you've gate-crashed my home, Miss Paget, I don't think the usual privacy rules apply. How are you planning to earn a living?'

She glared at him. 'If you must know, I'm writing a novel.'

'Dear God,' he said blankly and paused. 'Presumably it's for children.'

'Why should you *presume* any such thing?' Tallie asked defiantly.

'Because you're hardly more than a child yourself.'

'I'm nineteen,' she informed him coldly.

'I rest my case,' he returned cynically. 'So what kind of a book is it?'

She lifted her chin. 'It's a love story.'

There was a silence and Tallie saw a gleam of hateful amusement dawn in the green eyes. 'I'm impressed, Miss Paget. It's a subject you've researched in depth, of course?'

'As much as I need,' she said shortly, furious to discover that she was blushing again.

'In other words—not very far at all.' He was grinning openly now. 'Unless I miss my guess—which I'm sure I don't, judging by your terrified nymph act when I walked in on you just now.'

Tallie's blush deepened hectically.

Oh, God, I might as well have 'Virgin—untouched by human hand' tattooed across my forehead, she thought, loathing him.

He was speaking again. 'And you've actually staked your economic future on this unlikely enterprise?'

She was almost tempted to tell him about Alice Morgan. Make him see that it wasn't all pie in the sky but a calculated and considered risk, except that it was none of his damned business. And, anyway, why should she explain a thing to someone who'd already mortified her beyond belief and was now going to ruin everything else for her?

'Yes,' she said, icily. 'Yes, I have.'

'Well,' he said, 'that pretty well explains why you snatched at the chance of living here when Kit dangled it in front of you.' He paused. 'Are you paying him rent?'

She shook her head. 'Just—my share of the utility bills.'

'Which can be pretty steep for a place this size. So how can you possibly afford them?'

'By working day and night for months and saving every possible penny,' she said huskily. 'In order to give myself some dedicated time—a window of opportunity.'

'You seem to have mastered the jargon anyway,' he commented dryly as he refilled his mug. 'Where were you living before this?'

'I was sharing a flat,' she said, 'with my…my cousin and a friend of hers.'

'Excellent,' he said. 'Then you have a place to go back to.'

Tallie stared into her mug. She said with difficulty, 'No—no—I don't. I—really can't do that.'

She was expecting him to demand another explanation, but instead he said with a kind of damning finality, 'Then you'll have to find somewhere else, and quickly. Because you certainly can't remain here.'

She'd known it would almost certainly come to that, but hearing it said aloud was still a blow. Not that she intended to meekly acquiesce, of course. This had been the perfect haven until *he'd* turned up, and she wasn't giving up without a fight.

She said, 'But there is nowhere else. Besides, I was invited by your brother. I was relying on him. Does that make no difference to you?'

'None at all,' he said brusquely. 'And if you'd known him better— or used a little common sense—you'd have saved yourself a lot of trouble. Because Kit had no right to make such an arrangement with you, or anyone else. And, in future, he certainly won't be staying here either,' he added grimly. 'So Veronica can go hang herself.'

He'd mentioned the name before. 'Is that Kit's mother?'

'Unfortunately, yes.' His tone was clipped.

'Then perhaps I could speak to her about all this. Ask her to contact Kit and get it sorted out. After all, she must know that the flat doesn't belong to him, and she might help.'

His mouth curled. 'I don't recommend it. For one thing, Kit is the apple of her eye, and therefore can do no wrong. She would simply blame you for misunderstanding one of the dear boy's misguided acts of kindness.' His voice was cynical. 'Besides, she's always regarded anything with the name Benedict attached to it as communal property and encouraged Kit to do the same.'

He paused. 'And she would almost certainly regard you as some female predator in pursuit of him, and decide that he'd gone to Australia simply to get away from you.'

Tallie stiffened. 'That's ridiculous.'

He shrugged. 'Undoubtedly, but that won't stop her, and I can promise you that a penniless would-be writer isn't at all what she has in mind for her only chick. So I'd steer well clear, if I were you.'

'If you were me,' she said, 'you wouldn't be in this mess.'

His smile was reluctant. 'No, I wouldn't.'

'So what happens now?' She tried for nonchalance, and missed. 'Do I get thrown—bag and baggage—into the street?'

He was silent for a moment, his mouth compressed into grimness. 'How long have you been living in London?'

'A year,' she returned defensively, guessing what was coming.

'Long enough to make friends who might put you up on a temporary basis?'

She didn't look at him as she shook her head. She must seem absolutely pathetic, she thought. A genuine Natalie No-mates. Yet several of the girls she'd worked with had invited her for a drink after work, which might have been a first step to friendship. But she'd always been obliged to refuse because she'd been working and she needed to keep every penny of her earnings for the future.

And, of course, there was Lorna, friend from her school days, who'd help if she could in spite of the inconvenience, especially if she discovered Tallie was in dire straits. Only it simply wasn't fair to impose that kind of pressure on her, she told herself. No, she had to find her own solution.

'And before London?' He sighed abruptly. 'No, don't tell me. You lived at home with your parents, probably in some nice village full of nice people.'

'And if I did?' she demanded, stung by the weary note in his voice. He looked tired too, she realised for the first time, with the scar deepening the strained lines beside his mouth and the shadows beneath those amazing eyes, reminding her of the ordeal he'd just returned from.

My God, she thought. In a moment I'll be feeling sorry for him—if I'm not careful.

She rallied herself. 'What's wrong with village life?'

'Nothing, in theory,' he said. 'In practice, it's not the ideal way to equip yourself for life in the big city. Too big a jump to reality. Which is why I can't simply get rid of you, right here and now, as I'd like to do, because it would be like throwing a puppy out on to the motorway.'

Tallie gasped indignantly. 'How bloody patronising is that? Kindly don't treat me like a child.'

'Well, you certainly didn't appreciate my willingness to treat you like a woman,' he said softly. 'If you remember…' His voice died into tantalising silence and the green eyes swept insolently over her, as if the protection of the thick folds of towelling suddenly no longer existed. Making it hideously, indelibly clear that he hadn't forgotten a thing about their initial encounter, and might even be relishing the memory.

'So while you're still under my roof,' he resumed more briskly, 'patronage might be an altogether safer attitude for me to adopt. Agreed?'

Her shocked gaze fell away from his. Her brave words were forgotten.

She said in a stifled voice, 'I suppose…'

He nodded. 'And I know…'

There was another silence—tingling—charged.

Tallie's heart was thundering. She said quietly, 'Believe me, if I had anywhere—*anywhere*—to go at this moment, I'd already be on my way…'

'In that case, why not spend some of your savings on a train fare back to the village? Or don't you get on with any of your family?'

'Yes, of course I do. My parents are lovely.' She swallowed. 'But, even so, they wouldn't understand what I'm trying to do. Why I so badly need to see if I can finish this book and get it published. Actually make a career for myself as a writer.'

Mark Benedict frowned. 'Surely, if you explained to them…'

'It wouldn't work.' She spread her hands. 'They'd think I was being silly—living in a dream world—and want me to slot right back into the old life, treat the writing as a hobby—something I do when I've finished the day job. And that I can also put down at the drop of a hat when I'm needed for something else. Which I would be—constantly.'

She paused. 'But it just isn't like that,' she added passionately. 'That's why I know I have to stick to my original plan and stay in London. Although I promise I won't trouble you any longer than I have to.' She lifted her chin. 'There must be somewhere affordable I can live, and I'll find it, no matter how long it takes.'

'I wish you luck,' he said. 'I must also warn you that it had better not take longer than a week, my little intruder. Don't overestimate my capacity for philanthropy.'

She glared at him. 'Not,' she said, 'a mistake I'm likely to make.'

'Good,' he said, unmoved 'And, on that understanding, I want you and your belongings—all traces of you, in fact—out of my bedroom and bathroom within the hour. We'll discuss the other house rules later.'

Tallie bit her lip. 'I've been using your office to write in,' she said. 'Because there's a printer there.'

'Have you now?' His tone was cold. 'Egged on by Kit, no doubt?'

'Well, yes.' She looked down at her hands, clasped together in her lap. 'I have to admit a real work room was one of the flat's major attractions.' She sighed. 'I suppose he thought it was safe. That by the time you got back from Africa, I'd be gone.'

'No,' he said, 'he would have thought nothing of the kind. Even without the civil war, we'd have been on our way home within a few weeks. The project was nearly finished and he knew it. He also knew I wasn't expecting to find him here when I returned, because I'd already made it damned clear that I'd had more than enough of his freeloading and he could sling his hook.'

He shook his head. 'So I'd bet good money that he set the whole thing up quite deliberately. A serious piece of aggravation to await my arrival.'

'But I still don't understand,' she said. 'Why drag me into your private conflict? If that's what it is.'

'Oh, it wouldn't have been personal.' His tone was casual. 'I don't suppose he ever considered your feelings at all. You were just…a means to an end. A spiteful valediction to me before he removed himself out of harm's way.'

Tallie drew a breath. She said in a low voice, 'I've never been used like that before.'

'Well, don't worry about it.' He shrugged. 'Kit's just made you a member of a not very exclusive club.' He looked at his watch. 'And now I'd like to reclaim the more personal areas of my home, so perhaps you'd start moving your things. I'd like it all done before I go out tonight.'

'You're going out?'

'Yes.' He stretched indolently and got to his feet. 'As I mentioned before, I feel in urgent need of some rest and recreation.'

'But aren't you exhausted?' The words were uttered before she could stop them and she paused with a gasp of embarrassment as she encountered the glint of unholy amusement in his eyes.

'Not yet, sweetheart,' Mark Benedict drawled, 'but I certainly hope to be before the night is over. Any more questions?'

'No,' Tallie mumbled, her face on fire.

'Good,' he said. 'So maybe you'll shelve your gratifying concern for my well-being and do as you've been asked—please.'

Tallie rose too, her teeth gritted. There, she berated herself, that's what happens when you're stupid enough to feel sympathy for the bastard. So don't fall into that trap again.

She turned, heading for the door with an assumption of dignity completely spoiled by her unwary stumbling over the hem of the folds of towelling that shrouded her.

'Oh, and I'll have my robe back too.' Her tormentor's voice reached her softly. 'At some mutually convenient moment, of course.'

She found herself wishing with all her heart that she had the nerve to take it off right then and throw it at him, but such a gesture required far more chutzpah than she possessed, she realized, as she trailed, still flushed and furious, to the door.

Discovering, too, that some previously unsuspected female instinct was telling her without fear of contradiction that his mouth would already be curling in that nasty sardonic grin as he watched her departure.

Yet knowing at the same time that all hell would freeze over before she looked back over her shoulder to check.

CHAPTER FOUR

With her hair properly dried and severely confined with an elastic band at the nape of her neck, and safely back in her own clothing—jeans and a loose white overshirt—Tallie began to feel marginally better.

She could even be almost glad she hadn't slammed the sitting room door behind her as she'd been sorely tempted to do. But there wasn't any other cause for rejoicing.

She'd carefully collected all her clothes and personal possessions and transferred them to the spare room, before returning to the master bedroom to strip and remake the bed in its entirety, even down to the mattress cover, and choosing a dark blue satin spread as a replacement for the pale gold one she'd been using.

Then she'd gone over the room with a fine toothcomb to ensure that not so much as a tissue or a button had been left behind to remind him of her brief presence. She'd even dusted so there wasn't even a fingerprint of hers remaining on any of the surfaces, and she'd cleaned every inch of the bathroom.

He could do a forensic search and he wouldn't find me, she told herself grimly. I no longer exist in his space.

And at least he'd left her to it. She'd half expected him to stand over her, eagle-eyed, for any dereliction but, as far as she could gather, he was permanently on the phone in the sitting room.

No doubt telling a delighted world of his safe return, she thought, grinding her teeth. Or the female section of it anyway.

But she wouldn't think about that, she added with silent determination, turning her attention to the spare room.

Her new refuge wasn't as large as the one she'd just vacated, and the bed was much smaller—queen-size, she thought, instead of emperor, if there was such a thing—but it was furnished with the same careful, slightly old-fashioned elegance as the rest of the flat, and at least there was a table at the window she could use as a desk, she told herself as she retrieved her laptop and manuscript pages from the office.

And the wardrobes and drawers were empty, showing that Kit had taken his brother's eviction threat seriously enough to remove all his belongings.

Eviction…

The word lingered and stung, reminding her succinctly that her own tenure was strictly temporary and that she had just one week to find alternative accommodation. But could she do it?

Back to the evening paper, she thought with a sigh as she set about making up the bed, plus a serious trawl round very much cheaper areas—if there were such things in London—studying the cards in newsagents' windows. She'd probably end up paying a fortune for some boxroom where she'd be balancing her laptop on her knee.

However, even that would be bearable if it removed her from Mark Benedict's orbit, she told herself. Yet, in fairness, although it galled her to admit it, she could not altogether blame him for wanting her out of his home and his life. After all, he was entitled to his privacy.

And it was not his fault if she was left in an impossible and frightening position, but her own.

Oh, God, she thought, how could I have been so utterly gullible? But Kit was just so…plausible, insisting all along that it was a serious business transaction and that by accepting his offer I'd be doing him a real favour. Which was probably the only genuine remark he made in the whole affair. He just failed to explain the actual nature of the favour, she told herself ruefully. And he certainly never hinted that it could land me in any trouble—especially the kind of danger that a man like Mark Benedict could represent, she added, shivering.

But at least she hadn't been forced to spend the night in some seedy bed and breakfast, terrified to close her eyes in case she was robbed, although that comment about a puppy on a motorway still rankled.

But then almost everything about Mr Benedict grated on her, she thought, seething.

However—and here was the silver lining to this particular cloud—she needed a villain for her book. Someone rough, crude, dissolute, uncaring and generally without a redeeming feature, who'd make her hero's virtues shine even more brightly by contrast. And whose unwarranted interference in Mariana's life would involve her heroine in all kinds of misfortune and ultimately bring her to the edge of disaster.

But only to the edge, she thought, her heartbeat quickening. Because, in the end, it would be his own life that lay in ruins.

And Mark Benedict would provide the perfect template for such a man, his ultimate downfall and probable demise dwelt upon in painful Technicolor detail.

I'll make him so obnoxious that when he bites the dust the readers will be on their feet cheering, she resolved. And I shall gloat over every word.

It wouldn't be complete revenge, sadly, because her target would never know, but—hey—you couldn't have everything. And her own secret satisfaction would be all the compensation she needed.

And now, re-energised, she would see about her supper.

She marched cheerfully to the door, flung it open and stopped dead with a gasp, her face warming vividly as she confronted the villain himself, standing outside, his hand raised to knock.

He glanced past her, his brows lifting. 'I see you've settled in,' he commented acidly. 'Don't make yourself too comfortable, will you.'

Little chance of that with you around... Tallie thought it best to keep her instinctive retort to herself.

'And you look a little flushed, Miss Paget,' he added. 'Guilty conscience, perhaps?'

'On the contrary,' Tallie returned, her tone brisk. 'I thought I'd obeyed all your instructions to the letter.'

'Well, here's another,' he said coldly. 'From now on, you don't answer my phone. I've just had to spend a considerable amount of time trying to convince someone that I haven't moved another woman in here behind her back and that you're not "a friend", as you claimed, but a damned nuisance.'

'Oh,' she said airily, cursing under her breath, 'that. I...I'd forgotten.'

But she remembered now—particularly recalling the haughty voice of her interrogator and how it had needled her. Just like the harshness of his tone was flicking her on the raw now.

Two autocrats together, she thought. They're perfect for each other.

He was frowning. 'What the hell did you think you were doing?'

She sighed. 'Kit actually told me to say I was the cleaner if anyone rang, but it was incredibly late when your...your lady called, and it wasn't feasible that I'd be there doing a little light dusting in the middle of the night. So I said the first thing that occurred to me.'

'That,' he said grimly, 'is a habit you'd do well to break.'

'Consider it done,' she said. She paused. 'And I'm sorry if I injured your...real friend's feelings in any way, although I must say I didn't get the impression she'd be quite that sensitive.'

She took a deep breath. 'And I certainly hope she never finds out about your own little habit—sexually harassing complete strangers—because I'd say that leaves my own little *faux pas* in the shade—and might drive her into a total nervous breakdown.'

'Wow,' he said softly. 'The prim schoolgirl has quite a turn of phrase. But I think the lady in question would probably find it far more disturbing if I found a naked girl in my bathroom and wasn't tempted in any way—even if only for a moment.'

He added with cold emphasis, 'Also, sweetheart, one look at you would be more than enough to convince her that nothing happened between us.'

She stood staring at him, feeling as if she'd been punched in the stomach. First Gareth, she thought numbly, now this—bastard. Not only have I been totally humiliated by him, I now seem to be carrying the sexual equivalent of the mark of Cain.

Confirmation, as if I needed it, that no one could possibly want me.

Her throat tightened suddenly, uncontrollably as she fought to maintain her composure.

To hell with him, she thought shakily. Why should I give a damn what he thinks of me? If I've unfortunately failed to reach his required standard in female sensuality?

Besides, being regarded by him as undesirable has to be a positive advantage in the present situation, because at least I won't be spending the next few days and nights fighting him off.

That, she thought, is what I have to keep telling myself. And what I need, at all costs, to believe.

She swallowed. 'Thank you.' She added, 'That's—reassuring. Now, perhaps you'd go,' only to hear her voice suddenly crack in the middle and to realise that his tall, inimical figure had somehow become a blur.

Oh, no, she wailed silently, don't let this be happening to me. Don't let me cry in front of this uncaring swine of a man.

'Is something wrong?'

His voice seemed to reach her from the far distance. Tallie shook her head blindly and turned away, struggling to control the sobs that were choking her throat.

He said wearily, 'Oh, dear God,' and then his arm was round her, holding her firmly as he urged her across the room towards the bed.

She tried to pull away. 'Leave me alone.' Her shaking voice was thick with tears. 'Don't dare to touch me.'

'Now you're being absurd.' He pushed her down on to the edge of the mattress and sat beside her, handing her an immaculate white linen handkerchief before pulling her closer so that her head rested against his shoulder, and holding her there as deep, gusty sobs shook her slight body.

It was like leaning against a rock and Tallie knew, in some far corner of her mind, that, as soon as she'd stopped crying, she would want to die of shame for allowing it, because he was the last person in the world that she would ever want to see her like this, eyes blubbering, nose running, totally out of control.

Knew too that she should be pushing him away instead of blotting her wet face on his shirt. Telling him at the top of her voice that sleeping in a cardboard box would be preferable to spending even one more minute under his roof.

And he'd hear all that, and much more, if she could just… stop…crying…

She slumped against him, her tears fiercer and more scalding as she wept out her disappointment and hurt, her terrifying uncertainty about her immediate future, and her humiliated rage against the man whose arm encircled her like a ring of iron.

But, gradually, the tearing sobs began to diminish and the burning in her throat to subside, leaving a strange emptiness in place of the grief and anger. A vacuum that, slowly but surely, was being occupied by other, more insidious emotions. Feelings that she could not understand, let alone explain or justify.

She was suddenly, potently aware of the physical reality of the hard male warmth supporting her. Conscious that the comforting rhythm of his heartbeat under her cheek, the strength of his embrace and the clean, beguiling scent of his skin were all permeating her shaking senses in a manner as unfamiliar as it was disturbing. And that his other hand was stroking her hair back from her aching forehead with unexpected gentleness.

Like soothing a puppy abandoned on the motorway…

Tallie sat up abruptly and he released her at once, waiting in silence as she used his handkerchief to wipe her face and blow her nose. Mortified to notice, as she did so, that she'd left a damp patch on his shirt.

Eventually she said in a small brittle voice that still trembled a little, 'Please…excuse me. I don't usually embarrass myself like this—or anyone else, for that matter.'

'You didn't embarrass me,' he said. 'If anything, I feel guilty because it seems to be my comment on your obvious sexual innocence that acted as the trigger in all this.' He added quietly, 'However, what I don't understand is why that should be. Why you should feel insulted or troubled by my assumption that you're still a virgin, even if it could have been expressed more tactfully.

'After all, taking your time before you dash into some ultra-heavy relationship makes a lot of sense, especially these days.'

She kept her gaze fixed on the pale cord carpet. 'But not everyone sees it in quite the same way.' *And what on earth had prompted her into an admission like that?*

'Oh, dear,' he said, not unkindly. 'Has some callow youth been hassling you because you said no?'

'No,' she said. 'Not at all. It turned out that he…he preferred… girls with more experience.'

Oh, God, she thought, I can't be doing this. I can't be sitting on a bed telling Mark Benedict about my failed love life. And if he bursts out laughing, I shall only have myself to blame.

'Then he certainly won't have far to look,' he said caustically, the firm mouth surprisingly unsmiling. 'And you, sweetheart, have probably been saved a world of grief. Congratulations.'

'But I love him.' She hadn't intended to say that either, and her words fell with utter desolation into a silence that seemed to stretch into eternity.

She found herself stealing a glance at him, wondering, and saw that he was very still, gazing in front of him, the dark brows drawn together in a faint frown.

But, when he spoke, his tone was almost casual. 'Well, don't worry about it,' he said, getting to his feet. 'They say first love is like measles—lousy at the time, but conferring immunity afterwards. And one of these days you'll wake up and wonder what you ever saw in this crass Casanova.'

Tallie lifted her chin. 'Please don't call him that,' she said defensively. 'You know nothing at all about him—or me.'

'Agreed.' Mark Benedict nodded. 'And, where he's concerned, I'd find it hard to take an interest. But I'd bet there are a lot of girls out there who'll be waking up tomorrow in strange beds, feeling used up and disappointed, who'd like nothing better than to turn the clock back and find themselves in your shoes with life still waiting to happen.

'Besides,' he added softly, 'think how much more you'd have to regret if he'd taken everything you had to give and still walked away.'

'I'm sure your logic is impeccable,' Tallie said coldly. 'But it doesn't actually make me feel any better about the situation.'

Nor did it justify this extraordinary conversation either, she thought, or explain how she was going to live with herself after this unforgivable piece of self-revelation.

She was bitterly aware that she'd allowed him to get too close—physically as well as mentally, as if the room had shrunk in some strange way—and knew that she needed to distance herself—and fast.

Swallowing, she rose too, folding her arms across her body in a defensive gesture she immediately regretted. She kept her voice level. 'I—I'm sorry to have involved you in all this. It certainly won't happen again. And I know you're…going out tonight,' she added primly. 'So please don't let me keep you.'

The grin he sent her had 'wicked' stamped right through it and she felt her stomach curl nervously in a response as involuntary as it was unexpected.

'Don't worry, sweetheart,' he said softly, 'you won't.' He paused, his glance flicking past her to the bed and the pile of white towelling draped across the coverlet. 'But, before I go, I'll have my robe back.'

Tallie bit her lip. 'Shouldn't I launder it first?'

'No need for that.' He held out a compelling hand, leaving her no choice but to fetch it. 'It's hardly contaminated after its brief acquaintance with you. Besides,' he added softly, 'it holds memories that I shall fully enjoy savouring each time I wear it myself.'

And he walked off, leaving Tallie staring after him, her heart beating like a kettle drum, furiously aware that she was blushing again.

This coming week is going to seem an eternity, Tallie thought as she picked her way without noticeable enthusiasm through her cheese salad that evening.

And I have no one to blame but myself, she acknowledged sombrely. Why couldn't I simply apologise for annoying his girlfriend and leave it at that? Why have a go, however justified I may have felt it was at the time? Especially when all I've achieved by it is to make a spectacular fool of myself?

Well, I'll know better next time—except that I'm going to make quite sure there is no next time. A policy of strict neutrality plus a swift and unobtrusive departure is what I must aim for now.

She'd already checked to make sure there was a bolt on the inside of the door in the bathroom she'd be using from now on, and she'd take care that it was securely fastened on every visit— and that she'd be wearing her own elderly dressing gown too, she thought, her skin burning again.

And, eventually, she'd be able to put the whole sorry interlude behind her, and send Mr Benedict to the dump bin in her memory. With luck, she might even stop feeling as if her skin had been scrubbed all over with steel wool.

However, she told herself as she washed up her supper things and put them away, the positive side to all this was having the flat to herself again, at least for the evening, if not all night. So she could get back to her writing undisturbed.

If 'undisturbed' was really the word she was looking for.

Because, try as she might, Tallie found concentration difficult. Long after she'd heard the front door slam, signalling his departure, she discovered disagreeably, as she stared at her laptop screen, that her encounters with Mark Benedict were still occupying the forefront of her mind and lingering there to the detriment of the unfortunate Mariana, whose mule had somehow got free in the night and run off, forcing her to spend the day walking miles over rough terrain, until at last she came upon a stream that she could follow downhill.

Luxury—compared with the day I've had, Tallie muttered under her breath.

But eventually she became caught up in her story again, and when the sudden steep gradient of the track Mariana was descending turned the stream into a welcome cascade draining into a pool, Tallie allowed her hot, tired heroine to take off her boots and hide them behind a rock with the rest of her clothing and bathe her aching body in the cool water. A brief interlude amid the traumas of her journey when she could relax and dream about her eventual reunion with her husband-to-be.

Which might help make him more real—more desirable—as Alice Morgan had suggested, she reminded herself.

But as Mariana stood under the little waterfall, lifting her face to its fresh drops as if she was seeking the gentleness of William's lips, a man's harsh drawl invaded her paradise. 'A water nymph, by God. What an unexpected pleasure.' And, transfixed with horror, she realised she was no longer alone. That someone was watching from the other side of the pool, the sound of his horse's approaching hooves muffled by the rush of the water.

Hugo Cantrell, thought Tallie with immense satisfaction. That was what she'd call her villain. Major Hugo Cantrell—deserter, gambler, rapist and traitor. Maybe even murderer, although she'd have to think carefully about that. But dark, green-eyed, arrogant as a panther and twice as dangerous, with a soul as scarred as his face. Destined to be court-martialled and hanged. Slowly.

Her fingers were suddenly flying over the keyboard, the words pouring out of her, because this was Mariana's first traumatic encounter with him and she had to make it memorable—not difficult when she had all her own recent feelings of embarrassment and humiliation to draw on. And then she could slowly work up to the moment, building the tension, when Mariana would somehow manage to escape the threatened dishonour.

But how, with the evil Major Cantrell, now dismounting from his horse in a leisurely manner, his eyes appraising Mariana with an expression of lustful insolence that made her blood run cold?

Not that she'd be very warm anyway, standing stark naked under a waterfall, Tallie decided, doing a swift edit.

'Cool water and a pretty body.' His voice reached her, gloating. 'Just the kind of rest and recreation a man needs in the middle of a hot and dusty day.'

For a moment Mariana stood, paralysed with shock and growing fear, as she watched him tethering his horse to a tree, before stripping off his coat and sitting down on a convenient boulder to remove his boots.

Her glance slid to the rock where her own clothes were concealed.

Not all that far away, it was true, but certainly not near enough for her to reach them before he reached her. And how could she hope to outrun him—on foot and carrying her garments?

Somehow she had to devise a strategy, and quickly, because he'd stepped down into the pool and was wading purposefully towards her.

And then she remembered a piece of advice bestowed on her by her Aunt Amelia, her father's worldly younger sister. 'If you ever find yourself alone with a gentleman who is becoming altogether too pressing in his attentions, my dear, a severe blow with your knee in his tenderest parts will incapacitate him for sufficient time to allow you to rejoin the company in safety. And, naturally, having allowed his ardour to exceed his breeding, he can never complain.'

Not that the approaching brute showed any gentlemanly instincts, she thought with loathing as she forced herself to wait, eyelashes coyly lowered, as if suggesting that his presence, although unexpected, might not be entirely unwelcome to her. Because, if she was to achieve her purpose, she would have to allow him to come close, even within…touching distance. She had no choice, although the prospect made her stomach churn with disgust as well as terror.

As he got nearer, she saw that he was smiling triumphantly, totally sure of himself and his conquest. At the same time, she became all too aware of the power of his build, the width of his shoulders under the fine cambric shirt, and how the lean hips and long hard thighs were set off by the tight-fitting cream breeches, and felt a curious sensation stir deep within her that was entirely beyond her experience. Found herself wondering how all that total maleness would feel pressed against her when its covering was gone, and precisely how that hard mouth would taste on hers.

Realised, too, that a strange melting lethargy was overtaking her and that the drumming of the cascade was being inexplicably eclipsed by the sudden, wild throbbing of her heartbeat and the race of her breathing…

Hold on a minute, Tallie thought, startled, discovering she had to control her own flurried breathing as she dragged her hands from the keyboard. What the hell is all this? She's supposed to be about to do him serious physical damage, not melt into his arms. Have I just gone completely insane?

She read over, slowly, what she'd just written, eyes widening, lips parting in disbelief. Then, taking a deep, steadying breath, she put a shaking finger on the delete button and kept it there until the offending paragraphs were erased.

Mariana might be feisty and unpredictable, but she couldn't be stark raving mad. Because the entire plot of the book was her quest to be reunited with William, her one true love, and her body was intended for him and him alone. Which meant that even the merest contemplation of betrayal should be anathema to her.

Especially with someone like Hugo Cantrell, an utter bastard with no redeeming features whatsoever.

She does not fancy him, Tallie told herself grimly. She couldn't and she never will. Because I shan't allow it, any more than I'd let myself fancy that Benedict—creature.

Instead, she let herself elaborate pleasurably on the exact force of Mariana's knee meeting Hugo's groin, and the way he doubled up and turned away, groaning and retching in agony, exactly as Aunt Amelia had predicted.

Described vividly how Mariana made it to the bank and was already pulling on her clothing by the time he recovered and came after her, shouting she was a 'hell-born bitch', and, by the time he'd finished with her, he would make her sorry that her whore of a mother had ever given her life.

How he was far too angry and intent on his revenge to see the large stone in her hand until it was too late. How she hit him on the side of the head with all the force of her strong young arm, and saw him collapse first to his knees, before slowly measuring his unconscious length among the dirt and scrub at her feet.

Leaving Mariana to ascertain first that she hadn't actually killed him—because having the girl on the run for murder certainly wasn't part of the plot—then hastily complete her dressing and make her getaway on his horse, having discarded his heavy saddlebags because she was only a thief from necessity not inclination—and also because they might slow down her flight.

Her last action being to hurl his boots into the middle of the pool.

And that, Tallie thought with satisfaction, as she pressed 'Save' was altogether more like it.

And I only wish there'd been a handy rock in the shower earlier, she thought vengefully. Because there's not much damage you can do with a cake of soap, unless, of course, you can somehow get him to slip on it.

She dwelled for a moment on an enjoyable fantasy which dealt Mark Benedict a sprained knee, a broken arm and an even bigger lump on his forehead than Hugo's, leading hopefully to yet more scarring and a thumping headache lasting him for hours, if not days.

She sighed. She could get the better of him on the printed page, she thought wistfully, but grinding his face into the dust in real life was a different proposition, and so far he was way ahead of her on points.

And she mustn't forget that she'd come dangerously close to involving Mariana in a full-blooded love scene with his fictional counterpart.

Tallie bit her lip. That brief instant in the bathroom when she'd glimpsed him naked must have had a more profound effect on her than she'd imagined. And, disturbingly, it was still there, indelibly etched into her consciousness.

If only there was a delete button in the brain, she thought wearily, so that all my bad memories—all my mistakes—could be erased at a touch.

And then, with luck, completely forgotten.

CHAPTER FIVE

TALLIE emerged from the underground station and began the long trudge back to the flat, her feet whimpering in protest. She felt hot, sticky and dirtier than the pavement she was walking on, but she knew the sensation that her skin was crawling under her clothes was sheer imagination.

Nevertheless, the image of opening the cupboard under the sink in the bedsit she'd just been to look at, and seeing black shiny creatures scuttling for safety would lodge in her mind for a very long time.

It seemed to her that she'd spent most of the past week reviewing all the possible options. That she'd tramped endless streets, climbed endless stairs, and yet, in spite of her best efforts, she was still destined to be homeless in less than forty-eight hours.

Maybe I'm just too fussy, she thought wearily. After all, I can't exactly afford to pick and choose, not when time is running out on me. But everything remotely liveable is out of my price range, and in the places I might just be able to afford, I'd be afraid to close my eyes at night in case I woke up and heard hundreds of tiny feet marching towards me from the sink cupboard.

The only bright spot in her personal darkness was how little she'd seen of Mark Benedict since that first evening. In fact, he seemed to be spending the minimum time at the flat, which she suspected was a deliberate policy. That he was keeping his distance while he bided his time, waiting for eviction day when she would be out of his home and his life for good.

He was usually gone by the time she emerged from her room in the morning, which was her own deliberate policy, and he invariably returned late at night, if at all, so the rest and recreation season must still be in full swing.

Not that it was any concern of hers, she added hastily. And if Miss Acid Voice was the one to float his boat, then good luck to the pair of them.

Because the fewer awkward encounters she herself was forced to endure, the better.

Maybe, when the time came, she would simply be able to…slip away, leaving the amount she'd calculated she owed him for use of the electricity and the telephone on the kitchen table. A dignified retreat, with the added advantage that there'd be no difficult questions about forwarding addresses to deflect, and she wouldn't have to admit openly that she'd found nowhere else to live and that, as a consequence, she was going home.

In Mark Benedict's fortunate absence, Tallie had fielded two anxious phone calls from her mother that week, enquiring if she was all right and how the caretaking was progressing. She'd forced herself to admit there were a few teething troubles, adding brightly that she was sure they were nothing she couldn't handle.

Preparing the ground, she told herself wryly, for the moment when she turned up on the family doorstep confessing failure. And soon it would be as if she'd never been away, with the waters closing over her time in London as if it had not existed, and probably taking the book down with it too. Drowning it in loving routine and the domestic demands of a busy household.

Then there would be the rest of it. She could see her life stretching ahead of her like a straight, flat road. Finding a job locally, she thought. Running out of excuses not to go out with nice David Ackland, who'd joined his father's accountancy practice in the nearby market town, and who, her mother said, had been asking after her, wondering when she'd be back to visit.

And, hardest of all, trying to avoid all the places in the village that she would always associate with Gareth, even if he was never coming back.

The thought of him was simple misery—like a stone lodged in her chest.

But she had to get over it. Had to draw a line and prepare for her future, even if it wasn't the one she would have chosen.

Yet how many people are actually that lucky? she wondered drearily as she let herself into the flat, pausing to listen to the silence. Ensuring once again that she had the place to herself.

She dumped her bag in her room, kicked off her shoes and went straight to the bathroom for a long and recuperative shower, thoroughly scrubbing her skin and shampooing her hair until all lingering creepy-crawly memories were erased and she felt clean again.

She put on her cotton robe, bundled up her discarded clothing, and left the bathroom, only to walk straight into Mark Benedict in the passage outside, tall and dark in a business suit, his silk tie wrenched loose by an impatient hand.

'Oh, God.' Tallie recoiled with a gasp. 'It's you.'

He looked at her, brows raised. 'And why wouldn't it be? I do live here, in case you hadn't noticed.'

'Yes, of course,' she said shortly, annoyed at her overreaction, and wishing with all her heart that she too was fully dressed, with her hair dry, and definitely not clutching an armful of stuff that included her damned underwear. 'I was just…startled, that's all.'

'Well, not for much longer.' He paused. 'As I'm sure you're aware.'

'How could I forget?' Tallie tried a nonchalant shrug and found herself grabbing at her slipping bundle instead. Insouciance was never going to work for her with Mark Benedict around, she thought crossly. 'But please don't worry. I shan't exceed my deadline.'

'You've found another flat?'

'I have somewhere to go, yes.' She added with deliberate crispness, not wishing to be questioned further in case she let slip some hint that she was going home in defeat, 'If it's any business of yours.'

'You don't think I'm bound to be just a little concerned? Under the circumstances?'

'I think it's unnecessary.' Tallie lifted her chin. 'And please spare me any more references to abandoned puppies.'

'At the moment,' he said, his mouth twisting, 'a half-drowned kitten seems more appropriate.' He reached out and pushed a strand of wet hair away from her cheek with his fingertip. It was the lightest of touches, but Tallie felt it shiver all the way down to her bare feet. Found herself staring at him, suddenly mute with shock at her body's unwonted—and unwanted response.

'If you're still wondering why I'm home at this hour,' he went on casually, apparently unaware that she'd been turned to stone before his eyes, 'I have some friends coming to dinner tonight.'

'Oh.' She took a steadying breath, thankful that she hadn't been guilty of squeaking, jumping back in alarm or any other embarrassing giveaway. 'In that case, I'll eat early. Leave the kitchen free for you.'

'I shan't be slaving over a hot stove myself.' His voice held faint amusement. 'I use a firm of caterers—Dining In—but they'll probably be glad of some room to manoeuvre.'

'Naturally.' She managed a smile of sorts. 'Consider it done.'

'And when I have more time,' he said, his glance thoughtful, 'you can tell me all about your new place…Tallie.'

She was at her bedroom door, but she turned defensively. 'How did you know I was called that?'

'Because someone left a message for you on my answering machine earlier, and that's the name she used instead of Natalie.'

She flushed with vexation. 'Oh, heavens, my mother…'

'I don't think so. The name she gave was Morgan—Alice Morgan. She wants you to call her.' He looked at her curiously. 'You do know who she is?'

'Yes, she's the agent who's going to try and sell my book when it's finished.' Tallie took another deep breath. 'I'm sorry. I—I haven't mentioned to her yet that I'm moving, but I'll warn her…not to call here in future. You won't be bothered again.'

'For God's sake.' The amusement was tempered with exasperation. 'It's hardly a problem, if she needs to contact you. And why shouldn't I know that you're called Tallie? I've no objection to you addressing me as Mark.'

'Because Tallie's a private name,' she said coldly. 'Used only by my family and friends.'

Whereas, on your lips, it sounds as intimate as a touch, and I can't cope with that. Not again.

'From which I infer that I shall not find myself on your Christmas card list this year.' Back at a safe distance, he leaned a shoulder against the wall, folding his arms. 'Not very grateful when you've been granted a stay of execution.'

'But the sentence is still going to be carried out. Besides,' she went on hurriedly, 'I think it's much better if we remain on…formal terms.'

'However, even you must admit that formality's slightly tricky—under the circumstances.' His tone was sardonic and the green eyes held a glint that reminded her without equivocation that he knew exactly what her thin cotton robe was concealing.

She felt her face warm and cursed him under her breath. When she spoke, she kept her voice level. 'Circumstances that I did not choose, Mr Benedict. Now, if you'll excuse me, I'm sure we both have other things to do.'

Head high, she went back into her room, closing the door behind her with firm emphasis, then leaning back against its panels with a slight gasp as she tried to control the harsh thud of her heartbeat.

How did he do that? she wondered helplessly. How was it possible for someone she hardly knew to…wind her up with such ease? And why did he bother, anyway?

I'm still raw over Gareth, she told herself, which has made me more vulnerable than I should be. I ought to be able simply to shrug off Mark Benedict's crude, sexist jibes, instead of letting him see he can get to me.

But I can get back at him, and I will. While he's entertaining his friends this evening, I shall be busy with yet another encounter between Mariana and the revolting Hugo, and she'll be triumphing all over again.

She was smiling to herself as she dressed. In spite of her housing problems, she had to admit that the book seemed to be going really well, as she would be able to tell Mrs Morgan. And one of the reasons was clearly the introduction of Hugo the Bastard. In fact, she was enjoying Mark Benedict's character assassination by proxy so much that she might have to rein it in a little. Not allow him quite such a prominent role in case the gorgeous William appeared a little dull by contrast, which she could already see might be a danger, she thought regretfully.

But the battle of Salamanca was approaching, and he could play a starring role in that—leading a cavalry charge maybe, except that Hugo was probably the better horseman…

She bit her lip. Well, no need to mention that, and some judicious editing might be needed in other scenes. However, she thought more cheerfully, another couple of weeks and she'd have almost enough to show Alice Morgan as work in progress.

Or she would have done, if only the weeks in question remained at her disposal.

Come on, don't be negative, she adjured herself. At least you've got a long, uninterrupted evening ahead of you.

As she popped bread into the toaster and heated up a small can of beans for her supper, she found herself wondering if the snippy Ms Rest and Recreation would be among those present tonight. Not, of course, that it was any concern of hers. And even if the lady stayed over afterwards, the bedrooms were quite far enough apart to avoid any awkwardness.

Although any embarrassment would undoubtedly be all on my side, she admitted, chewing her lip again. What I have to learn is to be more relaxed about these things.

Not that it would matter once she was back under her parents' roof. They were old-fashioned about morality, and she supposed she'd inherited their attitude. Or thought she'd done so before Gareth had entered her life, she added with a faint sigh. If only he'd wanted her in return…

She ate her meal at the breakfast bar, then washed her plate and cutlery and put them away, making sure the kitchen was immaculate before she poured herself a mug of freshly brewed coffee to take to her room.

As she walked out into the passage, Mark was approaching from the sitting room, talking on the cordless phone.

'Look, don't worry about that,' he was saying. 'I'm just thankful that you and Milly are all right. No, it's fine. I can handle it. I'll book a table somewhere.' He listened for a moment, then nodded. 'Make sure you both get properly checked over. Goodnight, Fran. I'll be in touch.'

He saw Tallie and grimaced ruefully. 'My caterers,' he said. 'A car came out of a side street without stopping and ran straight into them. They're not badly injured, they reckon, just bruises and shock, but their van's a write-off and so, of course, is tonight's meal.'

'Oh.' Tallie stared at him. 'So what will you do?'

He shrugged. 'Try and find a restaurant that can feed six of us, although frankly I haven't much hope at this short notice.'

'Can't you cook something yourself?' She glanced at her watch. 'You've surely got enough time.'

'Sadly, I lack the skill,' he said. 'Eggs are my cut-off point—scrambled, boiled or fried. Hardly adequate under the circumstances.' His brief sigh held irritation and frustration in equal amounts. 'I don't suppose you number a chef among your London acquaintances—someone who'd like to earn a few extra bob before the evening shift?'

Out of nowhere, Tallie heard herself say, 'I can cook.'

There was a silence, then he said politely, 'I'm sure you can. What were you going to suggest—spaghetti Bolognese?'

'No,' she said. 'And you're being patronising again, just when I'm trying to help.'

She paused, then added levelly, 'In any case, a really good *ragu* sauce would take far too long to make. My mother's emergency stand-by dish—Mediterranean chicken with saffron rice—is much quicker, and it tastes fantastic. I suggest something really simple like smoked salmon for a starter, and a fruit flan from the deli round the corner as dessert. Chantilly cream would make it a bit more special.'

He said slowly, 'You're quite serious about this, aren't you?'

'You were entitled to throw me out a week ago,' she said, 'but you didn't. This makes us quits.'

Mark Benedict took a deep breath. 'Then I can only say I'd be eternally grateful. Write down all the things you need and I'll get them.'

Tallie raised her eyebrows. 'You mean you can cope with supermarkets?'

The green eyes glinted at her. 'Now who's being patronising?'

He took the list she eventually handed him, reading it through in silence, then glancing at her, brows raised. 'Anchovies? I don't think Sonia likes them.'

'Is that Miss Rest and Recreation?' The words were out before she could stop them. 'Oh, God, I'm sorry,' she added, flushing as she saw his mouth harden. 'It's really none of my business.'

'Hang on to that thought,' he suggested unsmilingly.

'Yes—yes, of course. And the anchovies dissolve in cooking.' Embarrassment was making her gabble and she knew it. 'Your—your friend won't even know they're there, I promise. Or me either, for that matter,' she went on hastily.

'You're planning to dissolve too?'

She bit her lip. 'No,' she returned stonily. 'Just maintain my usual low profile.' She paused. 'After all, you have to admit that I've hardly been obtrusive this week.'

'That,' said Mark Benedict, 'is a matter of opinion. But we won't debate it now because I have to go shopping.'

When he'd gone, Tallie went into the dining room. She found the elegant linen table mats and the napkins that matched them, gave the silver cutlery and the tall wineglasses with their impossibly slender stems a careful polish, and set places for six people.

There were three dinner services in the tall cupboards that flanked the fireplace and she chose the simplest one—plain white china delicately edged in silver. Because she couldn't be sure how long it was since it had been used, she tied a tea towel round her waist in lieu of an apron and gave the plates, cups and dishes a swift but thorough wash.

She was just drying the last piece when Mark Benedict returned.

'You've been busy,' he commented, pausing at the dining room door before joining her in the kitchen.

'You did say six people?'

He nodded. 'My cousin Penny, with her current companion, Justin Brent, two pals of mine, Charlie and Diana Harris, plus Sonia, of course, and myself.' He paused. 'Although, you are naturally welcome to join us,' he added courteously.

'You're very kind,' she returned with equal politeness. 'But I've eaten already.' *And even if I was starving, I'd still say no.*

She began to unpack the heavy carriers, almost disappointed to discover that he hadn't forgotten a thing.

'Is there anything I can do?' He was propped in the doorway, watching her, his presence making the kitchen seem oddly smaller and more cramped.

'No, thanks. It's all down to me now.' She hesitated. 'Although I wasn't sure if you'd want to use those lovely candlesticks on the sideboard, and whether or not there were any candles for them.'

'A romantic thought,' he said. 'But I think we'll stick to the wall lighting.'

'Just as you wish.' Tallie began to chop onions, praying at the same time that his frankly disturbing scrutiny wouldn't cause her to lose a finger. As she reached for the garlic press, she said with faint asperity, 'There's no need to stand over me. I didn't include rat poison on my list, so don't worry.'

'Do I give that impression? Actually, I'm simply admiring your efficiency.'

'And checking at the same time that I really know what I'm doing.' She gave him a steady look. 'However, I'm not accustomed to an audience, so if you're sufficiently reassured, maybe you could go and see to…wine and things.'

The firm lips twitched. 'Wine and things it is, then,' he murmured. 'May I bring you a drink, Miss Paget, to assist in your labours?'

It occurred to her that she felt slightly drunk already and that she had the way he'd been watching her to thank for it.

She said rather primly, 'I think I need all my concentration, thank you. But I do need some white wine for the sauce. Nothing too fancy,' she added hastily.

Mark Benedict gave an easy shrug. 'I was thinking of continuing the Mediterranean theme with some rather nice Orvieto. Will a slightly cheaper version do for cooking?'

She nodded, staring rather fiercely at the chicken joints she was extracting from their packaging.

'And please try to relax, sweetheart,' he added quietly. 'You're doing me a big favour, remember, not passing some crucial examination.'

Easy for him to say, thought Tallie. He hasn't got, *Don't mess up—don't mess up* unrolling through his mind like a banner as I have. And I lied when I said I wasn't used to an audience. At home, there were always people in the kitchen and it never bothered me. So why is it different with him?

But she couldn't answer that, any more than she could explain to herself why she'd volunteered to cook this meal. It had been an absurd thing to do, especially when she owed him less than nothing. She could so easily have left him to sort out his own dilemma—and been perfectly justified in doing so.

Yet, maybe, in some weird way, she'd wanted to prove to Mark Benedict that she wasn't simply a freeloader with grandiose ideas about her own talent and an aversion to working for a living. That she was, in fact, as practical as the next person.

Maybe she also wanted to show him that she was large-minded enough to overlook his past behaviour. Heaping coals of fire on his head, as the saying went, instead of pouring petrol over him and chucking a lighted match.

And now all she had to do was prove her point, she told herself, determinedly turning her attention back to the task in hand.

Within the hour, her Mediterranean chicken was flawlessly assembled and already sending out a mouth-watering aroma of tomatoes, garlic and wine as it simmered slowly in the oven.

The smoked salmon would be served with a simple lemon wedge, a watercress garnish and little rolls of paper-thin brown bread and butter. She'd already whipped up the Chantilly cream to go with the tarte tatin that Mark had bought, arranged a platter of cheese flanked by a bunch of green grapes at one end and some celery sticks at the other, and spooned a rich Colombian blend of coffee into the cafetière.

All that was left was the saffron rice, which she'd cook at the last minute.

She looked down at her plain top and boring trousers, wondering if she should change into a skirt, make herself rather more presentable for the arrival of Mark Benedict's guests.

Don't be silly, she adjured herself crisply. You're the skivvy. You belong in the kitchen and no one's going to give a second glance at what you're wearing. Least of all the host.

Promptly, at eight o clock, the door buzzer sounded and she heard voices and laughter in the hallway. Then, a minute later, she was joined by a tall, dark girl with an engaging grin. 'Hi, I'm Penny Marshall, Mark's cousin. I gather you're Natalie Paget, otherwise known as our saviour—rescuing us from the queue at the local pizza parlour.'

Tallie smiled back. 'I don't think it would have come to that.'

'But I'd like to have seen Sonia's face if it had.' Penny lowered her voice conspiratorially. 'It might almost have been worth it.' She glanced round. 'Is there anything I can do?'

'Thanks, but I think everything's under control.'

'In that case, why not come along to the sitting room and have a drink with us?'

Tallie moved restively. Picked up a spoon and put it down again. 'That's…kind, but I'd really rather not.'

'We don't bite, you know. Well, one of us might, but she's not here yet, so you're quite safe.'

Tallie smiled with an effort. 'I see. Do I take it that you don't like your cousin's girlfriend?'

'Let's just say that, for me, she comes pretty low down on his current list of playmates.' Penny shook her head. 'Mark, of course, is a total commitment-phobe, which is probably why he spends so much time abroad when he has good people who could take his place perfectly well.

'And he seems to have rounded up every female in London who shares his views—or lets him think she does, anyway. I think a few of them have their own agenda, much good may it do them. So if Sonia believes she's extra-special, she's fooling herself.'

Tallie became guiltily aware that she was paying too much attention to these indiscreet disclosures.

She said firmly, 'Well, I must get on.'

'But you just said everything was fine.' The other girl gave Tallie a coaxing smile. 'So come and meet the others, while the coast is clear.'

'It just—wouldn't be appropriate.'

'Because you happen to be doing the cooking? Oh, come on now…'

'No.' Tallie met the other girl's gaze squarely. 'Because I'm only staying here temporarily, and very much on sufferance, and Mr Benedict wouldn't like it.'

'My dear girl, it was Mark's idea, or I wouldn't have dared, believe me. He said you might be more amenable if the invitation came from someone else.'

Tallie bit her lip. 'And I feel that things are best left as they are.'

'Ah, well,' Penny said with a sigh, and walked to the door. Where she turned back. 'As a matter of interest—and because I'm irredeemably nosy—how do you come to be here? Mark's the last person in the world I can envision taking in a lodger.'

Tallie's smile was wintry. 'I'm the one who was taken in. The offer came from Kit Benedict, who made me think the flat belonged to him.'

'Kit the Curst, eh?' Penny gave a short laugh. 'Now, why didn't

I guess? Egged on by his ghastly mother, no doubt. Sticking like glue to Ravenshurst clearly isn't enough. It must really gall her to know there's another desirable piece of real estate that she can't stake a claim on.'

'Ravenshurst?' Tallie queried.

'The family home in Suffolk. Lovely old house where Mark was born, and was growing up perfectly happily until the frightful Veronica got her hooks into his father and played the "I'm pregnant" card.

'Which was bloody clever of her, because Mark's mother couldn't have any more children. My parents have said it was the most frightful, heartbreaking time, but after the divorce Aunt Clare put herself back together and bought this flat with some money Grandfather had left her. And she got custody of Mark, although he had to spend part of each school holiday under the new regime at Ravenshurst.' She grimaced. 'You can imagine what that must have been like.'

Tallie thought of the love and security she'd always taken for granted, and shivered. 'Yes—I suppose I can—almost.'

'And as soon as his father died, Veronica sold the house without reference to Mark, who was abroad at the time. She moved to London on the proceeds and had a high old time. Then, within six months she'd got married again—to Charles Melrose of Melrose and Sons, the wine people.'

'Oh,' Tallie said slowly, 'I see.' *So that was where Kit's job had come from.* 'Did Mark mind very much about the house?'

'He doesn't mention it. But I don't think his memories of the latter years were good ones.'

She paused. 'And he had another problem too.'

'And what problem is that?' Neither of them had heard Mark's approach but he was there, just the same, standing in the doorway, making Tallie wonder apprehensively how much he'd heard and, at the same time, be thankful she hadn't contributed her own viewpoint to the topic under discussion.

He'd changed, she realised, into close-fitting black trousers and a matching shirt, open at the neck and the long sleeves rolled back over his tanned forearms.

He looked stunning but dangerous, she thought with a sudden intake of breath. Like a panther.

Penny sent him a wide-eyed look. 'Why, the late Sonia Randall, of course. Can't you get her better-trained, darling?' She sent him an impish grin. 'Although I suppose punctuality's hardly her most appealing attribute where you're concerned.'

Mark reached for a tress of her dark curling hair and tugged it gently. 'Behave.' He looked across at Tallie. 'However, I do apologise for this delay. Will the food be ruined?'

'No.' She turned away, putting the jar of oregano back in the cupboard. 'It—it's very good-natured.'

'Unlike dear Sonia,' Penny added. 'So how is it she's joining us tonight at some point? What happened to Maggie? I liked her.'

'Working in Brussels for three months.'

'Well, Caitlin, then?'

'Got engaged to her boss.'

'Decided to cut her losses, eh?' Penny enquired dulcetly, then pulled a repentant face as she encountered Mark's cold glance. 'Okay, I'm sorry—I'm sorry, and I'll write out a hundred times "I must mind my own business."'

'If I could only believe it would work.' He paused. 'Have you persuaded Tallie to join us while we wait?'

Penny shook her head. 'Cinderella refuses point-blank to come to the ball. You seem to have turned her into a recluse—one of the few women in the world who finds you undesirable, cousin dear.'

He said dryly, 'Perhaps that's just as well, under the current circumstances.'

'You mean someone you can't send home in the morning?' Penny's eyes danced. 'Now there's a thought. And you've persuaded her to cook for you, too. What next, I wonder?'

'We're going to leave her in peace,' Mark said with great firmness. 'Before she misunderstands your warped sense of humour and walks out on me altogether.'

He looked at Tallie, who was standing in rigid silence, her face warming helplessly.

He said lightly, 'Tallie, I apologise for my female relative. There's no excuse for her.'

She found a voice from somewhere. Used it with an approximation of normality. 'I feel much the same about my brother.'

She watched them leave, heard him say something that she couldn't catch and Penny's gurgle of laughter in response as they walked away down the passage.

Stayed where she was, leaning back against the work-top, looking ahead of her with eyes that saw nothing.

Undesirable...

She tried the word tentatively under her breath. Was that really how she thought of Mark Benedict? Or how she wanted to think?

And found herself remembering with odd disquiet the way her pulse had quickened when she'd seen him standing in the doorway. And how her mouth had suddenly dried...

But I was startled, she told herself defensively. He gave me a shock by...suddenly appearing like that—as if he was some kind of Demon King.

On the other hand, he does it all the time, so there's nothing to get stirred up about.

All the same, she was sharply aware that the sooner she was away from this flat and out of his life altogether, the better it would be for her—personally if not professionally.

And, in spite of the warmth of the kitchen, she realised she was shivering.

CHAPTER SIX

ANOTHER forty minutes passed before the door buzzer signalled the arrival of the final guest.

'About bloody time,' Tallie muttered as she lowered the oven temperature yet again. Her chicken dish might indeed be good-tempered enough not to resent being kept waiting. She, however, felt no such obligation.

There was a murmur of conversation in the hall and then a woman's remembered voice rising effortlessly above it, pitched just right to reach anyone who might be listening, especially in the kitchen. 'Mark, honey, you're actually letting this waif you've acquired do the cooking? Are you crazy? My God, we'll be lucky if we don't all end up in Casualty having our stomachs pumped.'

If there was some way I could arrange for it to happen to you, and the arrogant Mr Benedict, without the other guests being affected, the ambulance would be already on its way, Tallie thought grimly. 'This waif' indeed.

'But I need drinkies first,' the newcomer added with decisive clarity. 'And I've brought some lovely fizz to celebrate the success of my most recent shopping expedition. Yes, darling, I absolutely insist. A few more minutes won't matter, for heaven's sake. You see, I heard this whisper that Maddie Gould wasn't terribly happy…'

A door closed and the rest of the revelation was lost.

Maddie Gould…Tallie repeated to herself as she took the

smoked salmon from the fridge and arranged it carefully on the plates before adding the garnish. Now, why does that name seem familiar?

She was still trying to remember when a voice from the doorway said, 'Can I carry anything into the dining room?'

Tallie glanced round and stiffened, her eyes widening. Because, for one shocked, ludicrous moment, it seemed to be Gareth standing there smiling at her.

But of course it wasn't. This man might be the same height, with blond hair cut in a similar, slightly dishevelled style and blue eyes, but there, she realised, the resemblance ceased.

He was built on broader lines than Gareth and his features were pleasant rather than classically handsome.

He said ruefully, 'Oh, God, I've startled you, and that certainly wasn't the intention. I was lured here by this heavenly smell of cooking.'

Tallie added the final bunch of watercress to the plate in front of her. She said coolly, 'You're not worried about food-poisoning?'

'Oh,' he said. 'So you heard that?'

'Wasn't that the intention?'

He pulled a face. 'Yes, of course. That's why I'm here, really—to make sure you haven't thrown a wobbly and dumped the whole meal in the bin.' He looked at her solemnly. 'Promise me you haven't—not when I'm starving.'

Tallie found she was smiling. 'No, you're quite safe.'

'I'm Justin Brent, by the way,' he went on. 'And you're—Tallie? Is that right?'

'My full name is Natalie Paget,' she said. 'But Tallie will do fine.'

'My sentiments exactly,' he said, and his own smile warmed he unexpectedly, making her wish she wasn't flushed from cooking, with untidy hair and still wearing a damned tea towel.

No, she thought. Not Gareth, in spite of the physical resemblance, but someone very different, with kindness as well as charm. Someone she could possibly learn to like, given the opportunity.

'Let's take in the starters,' he added, seizing a couple of plates and starting towards the dining room. 'Maybe other desperate refugees will realise and join us before I pass out.'

As Tallie followed him in, he paused, looking round the table. 'Six places? You're not eating with us?'

'No, I'm quite definitely below the salt this evening. My own choice entirely,' she added hastily as his brows rose. 'I'd already eaten when I volunteered to cook.'

'Wow,' he said. 'That's awfully generous of you.'

She said stiltedly, 'Well, Mr Benedict has also been very kind, allowing me to stay here.'

His mouth slid into a grin. 'And I'd say that response lacks real conviction. But Mark's an old mate, and if he's…wary about being used, then it's fairly understandable.'

'So I gather,' she said wryly, then paused as she remembered that her information had come from Mark's cousin. And that this man she was chatting to was Penny's—what? Partner? No, that wasn't it. 'Current companion' was the phrase Mark Benedict had used, whatever that meant.

And just being agreeable to the help did not make him available—something she needed to remember unless, of course, she was planning to take a leaf from Josie's book, which she would not dream of doing. Even if she looked halfway decent.

Your place, she told herself firmly, is back in the kitchen, cooking rice.

She made a business of looking at her watch. 'Heavens, I must get on. Perhaps you'd tell Mr Benedict that dinner is served.'

As she turned to go, her smile was brief and impersonal. And, she intended, final.

All the same, she found herself hoping, now that the dinner party was actually under way, that it would be Justin who'd bring the used plates from the first course back to the kitchen and collect the platter of chicken, in its thick delectable sauce of tomatoes, peppers, olives, with tiny spicy cubes of Spanish sausage, and the bowl of perfectly fluffy golden rice.

But of course—inevitably—it was Mark Benedict.

He looked at her, brows lifting. 'Is something wrong?'

'Not a thing,' she denied too swiftly, angry that she'd allowed even a glimpse of her disappointment to show. She indicated a pair of oven gloves. 'Be careful, the dishes are very hot.'

'Thanks for the warning.' His glance was ironic. 'I thought you'd prefer me to burn myself to the bone.'

She shrugged. 'But then you might drop something, and I've worked too hard to see my food end up on the floor.'

'I should have known,' he murmured. He picked up the platter with care, breathing the aroma with lingering appreciation. 'God, this looks fantastic.'

'I hope it passes muster.' She sounded prim, she thought as she busied herself taking the fresh plates from the warming drawer and putting them on the counter top.

Or maybe she was just being wary. It wasn't a small kitchen by any means, but once again his presence in a room seemed to make it shrink in some inexplicable way, making her feel as if she needed to edge round it, pressing herself flat against the units in order to avoid physical contact with him. Which was absurd.

Yet it was only when he'd finally departed that she felt she could breathe properly again.

She hadn't used all the wine in her casserole, and she poured the remainder into a glass and took a reviving sip of its cool Italian splendour. In reality, her job was done now, she supposed, but the missing caterers wouldn't have left the kitchen in a mess with used pots, pans, knives and chopping boards, so she wasn't planning to do so either.

I owe it to myself, she argued defensively, as she began to load the dishwasher. I want to see the thing through to the end. Everything like clockwork.

Besides, that wonderful glazed apple tart would be even nicer if it was warm, she reasoned, hunting for a pretty glass bowl to contain her whipped cream concoction.

And also, if she was honest, it would be good to rub Mark Benedict's nose in her thoughtfulness and efficiency. Prove once and for all that she was no one's 'waif'—least of all his.

An hour and a half later, with the kitchen totally restored to order, Tallie filled the cafetière with a thankful heart. Mission accomplished, she thought. She could now vanish to her room and set about rescuing Mariana from her current dangerous predicament, trapped upstairs in a Spanish inn, which was little more than a house of ill fame, while Hugo Cantrell played cards in the room below with a bunch of equally villainous-looking locals, thus blocking her only means of escape, and, even worse, as a prelude to sampling the charms of the ladies on the upper floor.

Which now, of course, included Mariana—someone he was unlikely to have forgotten after their encounter at the waterfall.

It was annoying how easily this heroine of hers kept going off at a tangent, she thought restively, when she ought to be focusing far more on finding William, the man she loved, instead of allowing herself to be sidetracked so easily. Especially when, yet again, that track seemed to lead directly to arch-bastard Hugo.

But then I can hardly allow the course of true love to be too smooth, she reminded herself, or there'd be no plot. And Mariana had managed to dodge him unnoticed on the last occasion, which meant there would have to be a confrontation between them now…

'We're a coffee cup short.'

Tallie jumped and turned to face Mark, who was standing in the doorway, realising she'd been too deep in thought to hear his approach. 'I'm sorry. I was sure I put out six.'

'You did, but we need another for you, plus a brandy glass.' He smiled at her and she felt the charm of it like the unwanted stroke of a hand on her skin. 'We're all waiting to drink your health.'

'I already feel fine, thanks,' she returned tautly, annoyed at her reaction. 'And, as I've now finished here, I'd prefer to go straight to my room.'

'I was hoping for a more gracious response.' The green eyes

narrowed. 'Not that it matters. You're coming with me to be properly thanked, even if I have to pick you up and carry you. Understood?'

It was as if Hugo Cantrell himself had suddenly materialised—walked off the printed page, she thought, aware that her heart was thudding like a roll of drums. And threatening to carry her—where? Off on his horse, thrown ignominiously over his saddle? Or across a darkened room to a waiting bed...?

She swallowed, then lifted her chin. 'Do you never take "no" for an answer, Mr Benedict?'

'I'd say that would rather depend on the question, Miss Paget,' he drawled, as he collected the extra cup and saucer. 'Now, shall we go?'

As she moved rigidly past him, he loosened the tea towel round her waist and removed it in one deft gesture.

And to offer any kind of protest would only make her look ridiculous, she thought, seething as she walked to the sitting room.

'There's nothing to be shy about,' he told her quietly as she hesitated in the doorway. 'You're the heroine of the hour.'

But not in all quarters, Tallie thought, as her eyes rested on the woman seated on the sofa facing her, who'd signally failed to join in the general round of applause at her appearance, and was now looking her over with eyes almost the colour of turquoise that missed nothing.

For the rest, she had hair like burnished copper cut in a severe bob, skin like milk, plus long legs and full breasts, emphasised by the black silk slip of a dress that she was wearing.

'I'm Di Harris.' A sweet-faced blonde girl with serene grey eyes came up to Tallie, smiling. 'And that's my husband over in the corner struggling to decide between armagnac and Drambuie. What terrible choices men face all the time.'

She put a hand on Tallie's arm and drew her unresisting into the room. 'Charlie says you have to give me the recipe for that wonderful chicken,' she went on, handing her a cup of coffee. 'And I'm to use bribery if necessary.'

Tallie flushed. 'It's really very simple.' She was about to recite the list of ingredients when she remembered the forbidden ancho-vies and paused awkwardly. 'I'll write it all out for you and ask Mr Benedict to pass it on.'

'Or you could come round and cook it for us yourself,' the other girl tempted. She looked around her, eyes dancing. 'I'm sure everyone here would like a repeat performance.'

'I hardly think the child's experienced enough for that, Diana.' Sonia Randall's tone was chilly, cutting across the murmur of assent. 'And if she's thinking of cooking professionally, her pre-sentation could certainly use some work. I'm not used to having my food just…thrown on to a dish. Also, she needs to hire help with the serving. It's ridiculous expecting the host to trail backward and forward to the kitchen.'

Tallie's flush deepened. 'That was Mr Benedict's own idea,' she defended. 'And I've no ambition to cook for a living.'

'No?' The supercilious gaze swept over her again. 'Then how do you earn your crust?' She added impatiently, 'I suppose you do have a job?'

'Not…exactly.' Tallie bit her lip. 'You see—I'm writing a novel.'

There was a silence, then Sonia Randall gave a harsh laugh. 'Yes, I do see. You and a thousand others, of course, who don't have this golden opportunity to meet socially with a commission-ing editor for a major publishing house.'

She paused. 'But if you've been persuaded to set me up so that this young woman can try and ingratiate herself with me, Mark darling, I assure you I shall not be amused.'

Tallie thought she heard Justin murmur, 'Now there's a surprise,' but she couldn't be sure. She couldn't be certain of very much at all—not when she felt as if she were a biological specimen pinned to a board for examination.

Mark said curtly, 'There's no question of any set-up. Tallie has no idea who you are, Sonia, or where you work. The topic has never been raised.' He added coolly, 'And I don't suppose she'd have mentioned the book at all if you hadn't started interrogating her. She simply doesn't discuss it.'

'Well, I'd like to talk about it.' Justin moved to Tallie's side. He gave her a coaxing smile. 'You must tell us what it's about.'

'Oh, spare us,' Sonia intervened impatiently. 'I'm here to relax, not take part in some…busman's holiday.'

'Yet you're always telling us you're looking for the Next Big Thing.' The ironic reminder came from Penny. 'This could be it.'

'I doubt that very much.' Sonia examined perfectly manicured nails, her expression bored. 'Anyway, there's no chance of it coming to me. Alder House only takes scripts recommended by agents.'

'Tallie has an agent,' Mark said quietly. 'Alice—Morgan, isn't it?'

'Well, yes.' Tallie bent her head in embarrassment, wondering at the same time how on earth he'd remembered that.

Sonia's head lifted abruptly and she studied Tallie again, her eyes sharpening. 'My goodness,' she drawled. 'I'd heard rumours that poor Alice was getting past it, and now it actually seems to be true.'

'But didn't you tell us earlier that she represents Madeline Connor, your latest acquisition?' Mark asked coolly. 'Presumably she was still sharp enough to negotiate that deal.'

Sonia's crimson lips tightened. 'She didn't have much choice in the matter,' she said curtly. 'Maddie really wanted to work with me.'

Whereas I'd rather be boiled in oil, Tallie informed her silently, taking a gulp of hot coffee. But I should have recognised that Gould is Madeline Connor's real name, because she rang up when I was in Mrs Morgan's office.

Sonia's gaze was still fixed on her. 'Have you read any of her books?'

'Yes, of course,' Tallie returned. She'd devoured all the emotional, sexy, modern blockbusters that epitomised Madeline Connor's work. 'I look forward to them.'

'And imagine you're going to be just like her, I suppose.' Sonia sighed. 'Alice really shouldn't encourage you in that when Maddie's her client.'

Tallie looked back at her calmly. 'She doesn't—because I'm writing something completely different.' She drank the rest of her coffee and put the cup down on the table. 'And now I should be getting back to it, so I'll wish you all goodnight.'

She flashed a swift smile at the concerned faces watching her—not including Mark Benedict, who simply looked amused—and walked to the door.

She'd just arrived at her room when Justin's voice reached her. 'Tallie—wait a minute.'

She paused reluctantly, waiting for him to join her.

'I've come to apologise.' His expression was wry. 'I feel responsible for all that, because I asked about your book.'

'It's not your fault. She had it in for me before she got here.' She drew a deep breath. 'What on earth can he see in her?'

Justin gave a faint grin. 'Believe me, that's a question no man would ever need to ask.'

'Oh,' Tallie said, flushing a little, remembering the voluptuous breasts revealed by the skimpy chic of the black dress, and the full crimson mouth. 'Yes, of course.'

'But, forgetting Sonia, and how I wish we could,' Justin went on, 'I'd be seriously interested to hear about your book. So may I call you—take you out to dinner one night next week?'

She didn't look at him. 'I really don't think that would be appropriate. Besides, I'm not even sure…' She broke off, biting her lip. 'Not that it matters,' she added with an effort. 'And now I must ask you to excuse me.'

She was aware of real disappointment when she closed her bedroom door behind her. He seems so nice, she thought wistfully, so how can he be propositioning me when he's seeing Penny?

She sighed. But then, what do I really know? she asked herself almost resignedly. Maybe two-timing is just a way of life for men these days. And, if that's how it is, I'm going to be spending a lot of my time alone.

She nodded, almost fiercely, as she crossed the room to her table and sat down in front of her laptop. Her vigil in the kitchen had been productive, and she knew now how Mariana was going to elude the advances of Hugo Cantrell, fuelled this time by his desire for revenge as well as lust, so doubly dangerous. It was going to be a terrific scene, she thought, and nothing Sonia Randall could say or do was going to spoil her belief in her story and her ability to finish it.

What happened to it after that was in the lap of the gods, but maybe she should warn Mrs Morgan that Alder House was definitely a no-no, she told herself, grimacing.

Determinedly, she relegated Sonia Randall's dismissive remarks to the outskirts of her mind and turned her attention to the job in hand.

The words seemed to be flowing out of her as she wrote, then rewrote feverishly, building the tension as frantic minutes passed, with Mariana crouching on the bed, the ancient, filthy bed-covering ripping like paper in her hands as she desperately tried to fashion it into a rope to lower herself from the tiny window. Knowing, as she threw it aside, that even if the fabric held by some miracle, it would still be inadequate, leaving her with a dangerous drop to the street below, and certain serious injury.

As she stared around her, looking for some alternative means of escape and realising it did not exist. As she thought of William, prayed absurdly for him to come and find her—rescue her—when she knew it was impossible because he didn't even know where she was and would never guess, even in his worst nightmares, that she'd ever embark on such a foolhardy escapade.

When he'd be encamped wherever Lord Wellington was and assuming that she was safe in her father's house, living for—longing for—his return.

Then the terror of hearing the sound of a man's boots ascending the stairs, stumbling a little because he'd been drinking, swearing softly in English in the voice she'd never forget.

Finding the darkest corner of the room and shrinking into it, trying to use the shadows for camouflage as the door was flung wide on its creaking hinges, and she saw him, standing there, his silhouette grossly exaggerated by the flickering light of the candle he was carrying.

His glinting eyes scanning the room—searching, and inevitably finding.

The gloating triumph in his voice as he said, 'The runaway nymph at last, by God. I've been waiting for this moment, my beauty, and here you are, the delicious end to a perfect evening.'

The way he crossed the room, his stride long and steady, as if the sight of her had rendered him sober and grimly, wickedly focused. How his hands descended on her shoulders, jerking her towards him, and the insolent sensuality of his mouth.

And as he bent to her, Mariana, struggling to push him away, her heart pounding unevenly, suddenly heard someone knock on the door...

Except—it wasn't supposed to happen that way, Tallie thought, staring in bewilderment at the words on the screen. There was going to be a diversion when the Spanish ruffians from downstairs, realising that Hugo Cantrell had been cheating them with marked cards, came looking for retribution, dragging Mariana away from him when he tried to use her as a shield, and enabling her to make her getaway while he went down like a fallen tree under the murderous barrage of their fists and boots, and his choking, agonised cries followed her as she fled.

It was the second, louder knock that brought her back to full reality. This was fact, not fiction. Someone was at her bedroom door, trying to attract her attention.

She glanced at her watch and stifled a yelp as she saw the time. She'd been working for almost three hours and, if it was Justin, back for another attempt at persuasion, she could only hope he was sober.

She opened the door warily and stepped back with a small, startled gasp when she found herself instead facing Mark Benedict.

'For God's sake,' he said, an edge to his voice, 'do you have to leap away every time you see me, as if I was a mad axe-murderer?'

'Do you have to come banging on the door at this hour?' she threw back at him shakily. 'I might have been asleep.'

'With the light on?' he asked mockingly. 'As a prudent landlord, I'd have felt bound to intervene.'

'Or getting ready for bed, anyway.' She glared at him.

'You mean undressed?' He grinned at her. 'My luck's never been that good, or not twice in a week, anyway.'

Do not blush, Tallie told herself stonily. Do not give him the satisfaction of seeing you embarrassed yet again.

'Is there a reason for this visit?' she asked coldly. 'Apart from checking if I'm wasting your electricity, of course.'

'I've made some hot chocolate,' he said. 'I thought you were probably still working, and might like some.'

She stared at him, her lips parted in sheer astonishment. 'Hot chocolate,' she said at last. 'You?'

He shrugged. 'Why not?'

'I thought you'd have preferred something more exotic.'

His grin widened. 'To match my taste in women? But you've only met one of them.'

And that was more than enough. The words hovered unspoken between them.

She said stiffly, 'Please believe your…lady friends are no concern of mine.'

'Bull's-eye,' he approved. 'I'd be so grateful if you could talk Penny round to your way of thinking.' He paused. 'But most men have a weakness for chocolate in some form or other, and I'm no exception. So, do you want yours or shall I pour it away?'

She hesitated, realising reluctantly how long it had been since that gulped-down coffee.

'Thank you,' she said stiltedly. 'It's…very kind of you.'

'Call it conscience,' he said, his mouth twisting. 'I should have known better than to put you in the same room as Sonia. Although the kitten turned out to have claws of her own,' he added musingly.

'We waifs learn to fight our corner,' she returned, adding, 'However, I'd still prefer not to encounter her again—or intrude on your privacy in any way.' And bit her lip as she met his sardonic look.

'You won't. She left when the others did.'

Deep within her, she felt a disturbing stir of pleasure at the news. She said coolly, 'She must be very disappointed.'

'Well, she's not alone in that,' he said. His hand casually cupped her elbow, guiding her, to her surprise, towards the sitting room rather than the kitchen. 'You dashed poor old Justin's hopes pretty finally.'

'What else did you expect?' Tallie wrenched herself free and faced him hotly. 'You may not care about your cousin's feelings, but I think Penny's lovely and she deserves better than her boyfriend trying to date another girl behind her back.'

'Well, we agree about one thing,' he said, closing the sitting room door behind them. 'Penny is indeed a great girl. But you've got Justin all wrong. He was Penny's escort tonight, but only because he's her See If I Care Man.'

Tallie sank down on a sofa, staring at him. 'Am I supposed to know what you're talking about?'

Mark was pouring chocolate from a silver pot. 'It's quite simple. Up until a few weeks ago, she was seeing a guy called Greg Curtis. Serious stuff, with talk of an engagement. Then Greg's former girlfriend unexpectedly came back from Canada without the husband she'd gone there to marry, demanding sympathy, attention and the place in his life she occupied eighteen months ago. With the result that, suddenly, his future with Penny was in the melting pot.'

'But that's awful.' Tallie's brows snapped together. 'She must be devastated.'

'Pretty much.' He handed her a porcelain mug full of steaming chocolate. 'But she's also a practical girl and she suspects this may be just a wobble, induced by some pretty intense emotional blackmail from the ex-lady.' He smiled faintly. 'And that he'll soon remember why he was so thankful that the beautiful Minerva eventually opted for someone else.

'At the same time, my cousin's not the type to wear her heart on her sleeve, or sit round waiting while Greg sorts himself out. If he ever does, of course,' he added, frowning. 'However, for her own self-respect, she needs to be seen out and about with an attentive man in tow so that Greg will get the message loud and clear. Hence Justin, an old friend of mine, who has some bruises of his own and isn't looking for a heavy relationship right now.'

'Making him Penny's See If I Care Man,' Tallie repeated slowly.

I wish I'd found someone like that, she thought wistfully, when Gareth dumped me. So much better than moping around like a wet week, letting everyone see how much it mattered. As it is, I'll always feature as some naïve saddo. Not least with the man facing me now.

'But Pen doesn't have exclusive rights, if that's what you're afraid of.' Mark was watching her over the top of his mug. 'Plus, he's a nice guy and it would do you good to go out—flutter your wings a little.'

He paused. 'After all, you know what they say about all work and no play.'

'I have heard it before,' she admitted tautly. 'But even if Justin isn't messing Penny about, it makes no difference. I—I shan't be accepting his invitation. And I'll take my drink to my room, if that's all right.'

'It isn't,' he said laconically. 'To use a cliché—we need to talk.'

She lifted her chin. 'If it's about Justin, it's pointless.'

'May I know why?'

'I'd have thought it would be obvious—especially to you.' She shrugged. 'I'll be moving very soon. End of story.'

'But I'd be happy to pass on your new address.' Those amazing green eyes were watching her steadily. 'Except, of course, you don't have one—do you? Because you haven't been able to find anywhere else to live in London. Isn't that the truth of it?'

She looked down at her hands, clasped round the mug. 'No.' It hurt to have to admit her failure and to him of all people. 'No, I haven't.'

'So what are you planning to do?'

She hunched a shoulder, still not looking at him. 'Go back to my parents' home.'

'But that isn't what you want.'

'I don't really have any other choice.'

He nodded. 'And, of course, you think Justin may hesitate over pursuing you back to whatever rural fastness you came from.'

'It's hardly likely.' The fragrant chocolate was smooth comfort against the sudden tightness in her throat. 'But, as we've only just met, it's not a major concern. And I'm sure someone as attractive as Justin won't feel too put out.'

'Possibly not.' He was leaning back against the cushions, those endless legs stretched out in front of him, his gaze meditative. 'But it seems a pity to reject him out of hand. So why don't you forget the looming deadline for your departure and stay on here?'

She almost spilled her chocolate. 'Stay—here?' Her voice was hoarse.

'Why?'

'Because I think you deserve a chance.'

Her mind was reeling. 'With—Justin?'

'No, to finish your book, you little idiot. Your love-life's your own business. But you need peace and quiet in which to work, and I can provide that.' He paused. 'Besides, I'm seriously grateful about tonight.'

'But I already said—we're quits.'

'Well,' he said, 'maybe I'll ask another favour some time, if that makes you feel better.'

She wasn't sure how it made her feel, so she sipped at her chocolate as she tried to collect her random thoughts.

Eventually, she said, 'I don't think Miss Randall will be very pleased when she finds out.'

He shrugged. 'Why should she care? You're being invited to continue your occupation of my spare room, sweetheart, not move into my bed.'

The muscles in her chest seemed to clench oddly. She had to control her voice. 'But you don't want me here. You've made that clear.'

'I won't be here a great deal myself. I have several trips abroad coming up, and maybe a flat-sitter isn't such a bad idea.' He smiled at her. 'And you like the place, don't you? I've noticed the way you move round it—the pleasure with which you look at things—handle them as if they were precious.'

She tried for lightness. 'I didn't realise I was under such close observation.'

'Security.' He echoed her tone. 'I had to be sure you weren't a burglar's moll.'

He finished his chocolate. 'So—are you going to stay? I'm offering the same terms as Kit.'

She hesitated. 'In that case, yes, please.' She tried a smile. 'Although I could always cook you the occasional meal.'

He shook his head. 'This evening was a one-off. Same roof—separate lives. That's the deal.'

'Of course.' She put down her empty mug and rose. 'In that case, thank you, Mr Benedict, and...I wish you goodnight. It seems it's my turn to be grateful.'

'One other thing.' As she reached the door, his voice halted her. 'My name is Mark. Think you can remember that?'

She said huskily, 'I...can try.'

And, as she went away from him, down the passage to her own room, she found herself wondering if she'd found the perfect solution to her problems—or just made the biggest mistake of her life. She realised she could not find an answer.

CHAPTER SEVEN

TALLIE woke the next morning, uneasily aware that she was still unsure whether she'd made the right decision.

She sat up slowly, looking round her tranquil, sun-filled room, telling herself it was perfect—the ideal working environment. Reminding herself how much she'd written there over the past week in spite of everything.

Why, even last night, instead of going straight to bed, she'd sat down and finished the scene she'd been working on, although not in the way she'd originally intended, she admitted wryly.

Because after The Kiss which Hugo Cantrell had inflicted on the kicking and struggling Mariana, they'd been interrupted by the sound of feet thundering up the rickety stairs and furious voices baying for blood. And, instead of using her as his shield, Hugo had inexplicably picked Mariana up in his arms and strode with her to the window.

'Here.' He pushed a leather purse heavy with coins into her hand. 'My winnings. Now, go while you can, because they won't spare either of us.'

And, before she could scream in protest, he'd pushed her slender body through the narrow casement, dropping her into a hay-wagon passing below.

And as she lay, winded but otherwise undamaged, she heard from the inn the crashing of splintering wood and the chilling sound of a man shouting in pain.

That, at least, was what she'd originally planned.

Well, maybe even the nastiest pieces of work had their moments of weakness, Tallie conceded reluctantly. As Mark Benedict had surprisingly demonstrated last night.

But even if she'd let Hugo slip out of character for a few minutes, and she wasn't sure why that had happened, he was still the villain of the piece and nothing was going to change that.

And Mariana was definitely not going to return at some point, to find him broken and bleeding, so that she could bandage up his injuries with her torn-up petticoat and nurse him back to health in some remote barn.

Because any spare petticoats she had would be devoted to William, wounded during his gallant actions at Salamanca, probably by a sabre cut during Le Marchant's charge, she thought. Because he was the hero, and she must make sure the reader knew it.

But it was last night's decision that was still at the forefront of her mind as she showered and dressed. The flat seemed deserted when she emerged from her room, and for a moment she thought Mark had already left to pursue whatever he'd got planned for the day, but then she detected the murmur of his voice from behind the closed door of his office.

She was in the kitchen, just finishing her tea and toast when he came striding in, dark brows drawn together in a frown and his mouth set grimly.

Not a good sign, thought Tallie with sudden apprehension. Maybe she wasn't the only one having second thoughts about their new agreement. And it might be better to jump before she was pushed.

She said quietly, 'If you've changed your mind about letting me stay, I quite understand.'

'What?' He seemed to become aware of her for the first time. 'God, no. I've something else on my mind entirely.' He refilled the mug he was carrying from the percolator and leaned back against the counter top. He was wearing beautifully cut jeans and a plain white shirt, open at the throat, its sleeves turned back over his tanned forearms.

He said abruptly, 'I hadn't intended to ask so soon, but I rather need that favour I mentioned last night. It seems my stepmother is paying me a visit.'

'And you want me to cook lunch for her?'

'No,' he said. 'Just to be here. She claims she's coming on a business matter and I need backup.'

She hesitated. 'What do you mean exactly?'

'I mean I'd prefer not to be alone here when she comes calling.' His tone was blunt.

'Oh,' she said, as unwelcome light dawned, 'so that's what…' And stopped, flushing guiltily.

'That's what Penny was undoubtedly about to tell you when I interrupted,' he supplied, his face lightening into amused resignation. 'Are there any details of my life my dear cousin has withheld? For instance, did you get a recital of my childhood ailments, including how she gave me chickenpox when I was thirteen?'

'No—' Tallie's own mouth quivered into amusement '—but she might be saving that for another time.' She put her used breakfast things carefully into the dishwasher. 'So you want me to play gooseberry, is that it?'

'Not exactly,' he said carefully. 'I want you to pretend that you're my girlfriend, and that we're sharing a damned sight more than just our living space.'

She bit her lip. 'But surely you shouldn't be asking me. It ought to be…Miss Randall, or someone…'

'Actually, no.' A sardonic note entered his voice. 'I've no wish to send out misleading signals to Miss Randall—or anyone.' He paused. 'And as you and I have nothing going for us apart from an uneasy truce, that makes you the ideal choice.'

He looked at her. 'So, will you do it?'

'I…don't know.' She glanced down at the workaday jeans and top she was wearing. 'I hardly look the part of anyone's live-in lover, least of all yours.'

'That can be fixed.'

'And I'm not a very good actress.'

'Pretend it's a scene from this book of yours,' he said casually, and Tallie bit her lip, wondering if that wasn't a little too close for comfort.

'Very well, then,' she said. 'I'll do my best. What time is she getting here?'

'Mid-morning, she tells me.' His mouth twisted. 'And, as she appears to want something, she may even be on time.'

'Fine.' She summoned a smile. 'Then I can get some work done while I'm waiting.'

But an hour later she couldn't pretend she was satisfied with what she'd produced. Even while hurling himself on the French lines, William still seemed oddly remote. Maybe he would become warmer, more human, when Mariana came back into his life, she thought, and the sooner the better.

But maybe she was just tired. She hadn't slept very well the previous night, her mind invaded by disjointed words and images. 'Mark, of course, is a total commitment-phobe'...Mariana struggling in the arms of a man she hated, and, more than once, Mark's voice asking, 'Why don't you...stay on here?' And herself, fighting to find a reason and put it into words.

She was reluctantly saving what she'd written when there was a rap at her door.

'Come in.' She got to her feet, wondering apprehensively if she was being summoned because Veronica had arrived ahead of time.

But Mark walked in alone. 'I've brought you something.' He tossed a couple of carrier bags emblazoned with the name of a well-known department store on to her bed. 'I hope it all fits. I'm not intimately acquainted with your measurements, so I had to guess.'

Tallie opened the first bag, extracting a deceptively simple cream skirt and a scoop-necked silky top the colour of horse chestnuts. The second held a pair of high-heeled cream sandals.

When she could find a voice, she said, 'You bought these—for me?'

'I hardly plan to wear them myself. I suggest you change into them now. Practise walking in those heels.'

She gasped. 'I'll do nothing of the kind.' She tried to stuff everything back into the bags. 'You have no right—no right at all…'

He sighed. 'Please don't fuss. You admitted yourself you're not dressed for the part. Now you can be.'

She said, 'I could live for a month on what you've just paid for this stuff.'

Mark shrugged. 'Then tomorrow you can sell it on eBay,' he returned. 'But I suggest that you hang on to it. Wear it when you meet your publishers. You might get a better deal if they think you're not hungry.' He looked her over. 'And leave your hair loose.'

She was quivering with temper. 'Any other instructions—sir?'

'Not at the moment, but that could change.' He glanced at his watch. 'I'm going to put some coffee on while you get dressed. We haven't got all day.'

As he went to the door, she said, 'One thing occurred to me.' She hesitated. 'You don't think Kit may have told her about moving me in here? That she might recognise my name?'

'Unlikely,' he said. 'Even if he did share the joke with her, your actual identity would be far too unimportant a detail to mention.'

'Oh,' she said with false brightness, 'that's all right then.'

'No,' he said, more gently. 'But I'm afraid it's as good as it gets, with that precious pair.' He grimaced. 'As you're about to find out,' he added, and went.

The new clothes, she had to admit, were becoming. Even more annoyingly, they were a perfect fit. And the sandals made her already slim legs racehorse-slender.

She found herself wondering what Mark would say when she went to join him in the sitting room, but he merely looked her over, then nodded abruptly.

And a moment later the imperious sound of the buzzer announced that their visitor had arrived.

Tallie turned to him, apprehension twisting inside her. 'Shall I—answer the door?'

'We'll do it together,' Mark said. 'And—relax,' he added as they walked down the passage. 'Remember you're not here to make a good impression.'

The woman confronting them on the doorstep was tall and stunningly attractive, with blonde hair caught back in an immaculate chignon. Her complexion was flawless, her nose short and straight, and she had enormous blue eyes fringed by curling lashes heavily enhanced by mascara. Her reed-slender figure was moulded closely by a suit in royal blue, the skirt displaying shapely legs and the short jacket revealing rather more than a hint of cleavage.

Tallie, who'd been expecting a hatchet-faced harridan, found herself almost gaping. Kit's mother? she queried in silent incredulity. She doesn't look old enough.

She thought of her own mother—warm, pretty and adored by her husband, but with comfortable curves, a few first touches of grey in her hair and laugh lines around her eyes and mouth. Tried to imagine her in an outfit like that, and failed utterly.

'Mark, darling, how wonderful to see you.' Veronica Melrose's voice was low and husky. The astonishing blue eyes rested on Tallie. 'And who is this?'

'This, my dear Veronica, is Natalie.' He put an easy arm round Tallie's shoulders and drew her against him, giving her no option but compliance, she realised mutinously. But she could hardly accuse him of taking advantage of the situation when she'd agreed to this charade.

She was also aware that the older woman's harebell gaze had carried out a lightning assessment of everything she was wearing, costing it to the last penny. But she still wasn't sure she'd passed muster.

I'm just not glamorous enough, she thought, and swallowed.

'Do come in,' Mark went on. 'May we offer you some coffee?'

'That would be pleasant.' Mrs Melrose walked into the sitting room and deposited herself decoratively on the sofa. Not many women of her age could pout and get away with it, thought Tallie, but she managed it somehow. 'I did hope that our conversation would be a private one. Is there any reason for your…little friend to be present?'

Mark looked surprised. 'She lives here,' he said. 'With me. Perhaps I should have made that clear.'

'Perhaps you should.' The husky voice had acquired a metallic edge. She gave a little laugh. 'Well, well. The eternal bachelor caught at last. And in such a young and charming trap. How fascinating.'

Tallie said coolly, 'I don't think Mark feels particularly trapped. I'll fetch the coffee.'

'You seem to have made yourself quite at home,' Veronica commented as she returned, placing the tray on the table. 'Although you clearly haven't had a chance to put your own stamp on it yet—whatever that might be.' As she accepted the coffee Tallie handed to her, she flicked a disparaging glance round the room. 'But it so needs updating.' She looked at Mark. 'Kit told me he was astonished you hadn't brought in a decent decorator by now.'

'And is he equally amazed by Australia?' Mark enquired politely. He reached up a hand and pulled Tallie down on to the sofa beside him. 'I assume you've heard from him.'

'Indeed I have.' Veronica jerked upright as if a steel pole had suddenly replaced her spine. 'He's been telephoning me nearly every day. He's having the most appalling time, stuck at this vineyard which seems to be miles from anywhere else. The weather's disgusting—apparently it's winter—and he actually saw a snake.'

She shuddered. 'He should never have gone there.' She gave Mark a look that wasn't remotely seductive. 'But I have you to thank for that.'

'Difficult to see how,' he returned indifferently. 'When I was at the back of beyond myself, and in a totally different continent. Besides, didn't you sweet-talk poor Charles into taking him on at Melrose and Sons?'

Her crimson mouth tightened impatiently. 'I meant Kit should have taken his rightful place by now in his father's company.'

'I didn't tell him to abandon his engineering course at university,' Mark said shortly. 'That was all his own idea. But if he'd stuck to it, he'd have found himself in places he'd have liked even less than Australia.'

'There must be projects in this country too.' She waved a vague hand. 'Hotels, leisure complexes, shopping malls. Something he could have enjoyed.'

'But we're committed to roads, bridges and hydro-electric schemes,' Mark said gently. 'Long-term developments which will help rather more people.'

Veronica shrugged. 'Until they choose to blow them up, of course.' She added with a touch of malice, 'Isn't that what happened on your last site?'

'A temporary set-back,' Mark drawled. 'And now that the fighting seems to be over, we'll be going back to the Ubilisi to finish what we started.'

Tallie stared at him. When she spoke, she found her voice was shaking. 'But that's dangerous, surely. The previous government's been overthrown, and the new regime tried to kill you when you were there before. You only just got out last time.'

There was an odd silence, then Veronica gave a tinkling laugh. 'Why, Mark, the child is seriously concerned about you. How terribly sweet.' She looked at Tallie. 'But a complete waste of time, my dear. Mark is a law unto himself, and he actually revels in charging off to remote corners of the globe, turning disasters into triumphs. No one woman could possibly offer a viable alternative to that sort of buzz.'

She paused. 'But that does not mean Kit has to do the same. He can't possibly stay where he is, when he's so wretched. He needs to come home, and find work in this country.'

She paused again. 'So, I thought you might offer him a job. It's full time he learned about the company, especially when you're still hurling yourself into the world's trouble spots. After all, Kit is your nearest male relative, and if something were to…happen, he'd be your heir.'

'You think so?' Mark's tone was dry. He slid his arm round Tallie's waist, smiling down at her. 'But all that might change very soon.'

'Good God.' Veronica's eyes swept over Tallie's slim figure with disbelief. 'You mean…'

'I mean nothing yet,' Mark returned easily, as Tallie sat rigidly beside him, not knowing where to look. 'But we're working on it.' He paused. 'And there are no vacancies at Benedicts that would pay Kit the kind of salary he'd clearly expect, or make use of his extremely limited skills.

'We market our expertise, Veronica, trouble-shooting difficult engineering projects all over the world. Believe me, your son is better off where he is. And, if he works, he might even get promotion eventually.'

'I see.' The coffee cup rattled in its saucer as Veronica replaced it on the table. 'Then there's nothing more to be said.' Her look lasered Tallie. 'However, I do hope you're going to make up for my disappointment by offering me a bed for the night. I'm dining with friends this evening and I have an early dental appointment tomorrow morning.' She looked from one to the other. 'You do have a spare room? I'm sure Kit has mentioned it.'

'I'm certain he has.' Mark shrugged. 'But Natalie's currently using it as an office. Besides, I thought you always stayed at The Ritz.'

'I do, but Charles is being very difficult at the moment. Says we have to cut back on our spending.' The pout reappeared and the blue eyes rested smilingly on Mark. 'I didn't think you'd begrudge me just one night.'

'Except,' Mark said gently, 'that Natalie and I are enjoying our privacy, and really don't wish it to be interrupted, not even by the most understanding guest.'

'My dear Mark—such unwonted concentration on one woman. I can hardly believe my ears. I think the best thing I can do is go, and leave you in peace.' At the door, she turned. 'And please don't worry. There'll be other nights, I'm sure.'

When Mark returned from showing her out, Tallie was still seated on the sofa, staring into space.

She said, 'That was awful.'

'It's also over.'

'Is it?' She looked up at him. 'Your stepmother doesn't seem to think so. If I was genuinely involved with you, I'd be starting to wonder.'

'But as you're not,' he said coldly, 'you need not concern yourself.' He picked up the coffee tray and carried it to the kitchen. After a moment or two, she followed.

'I'm sorry.' Her voice faltered a little. 'That was wrong of me. I don't really believe that…you…that you and Veronica…'

'Thanks for the vote of confidence.' His tone was dry. 'It's slightly gutting to find someone thinks you can be that much of a bastard.'

'Yes.' The word had a hollow ring, the image of Hugo Cantrell large in her mind.

'Well, don't look so stricken.' His mouth twisted. 'Because I'm no saint, and at times it's been a damned close-run thing. Veronica can pack quite a punch, especially when you're sixteen and not nearly as sexually experienced as you like to think.'

Tallie gasped. 'She came on to you—at that age?'

'She'd correctly figured I wasn't a virgin. Also, she was only nineteen when she married my father, and he was already in his mid-forties. Maybe that side of their relationship was on the wane, or perhaps she was simply feeling the seven year itch.'

He paused. 'I've wondered since if she also saw it as a way of establishing a hold over me—insurance for the future, perhaps.'

He added lightly, 'On the other hand, she may simply have found the idea amusing. All those raging adolescent hormones at her disposal—if I'd proved amenable.'

'But surely she can't still think…'

'No?' he asked. 'When you admitted you began to wonder.' He shook his head. 'Veronica is not a woman to allow her marriage vows to stand in her way.'

'She's vile.'

'She's also sad.' He paused. 'But thank you for saving me from a potentially awkward situation. I owe you big time, and I won't forget it.'

'I wish I could say it was a pleasure.' She got to her feet. 'And now I have some awkward situations of my own to deal with, so I'd better get back to work.'

'You won't allow me to express my gratitude by taking you for an expensive lunch? It seems a pity to waste the new gear.' His voice followed her to the door.

She didn't look back at him. 'No, thanks.' She sounded faintly brittle. 'Veronica seems to have killed my appetite stone dead.'

Back in her room, she found she was leaning back against the panels of the door, panting as if she'd been running, angry with herself and bewildered at the same time. After all, she was undeniably hungry, so where would have been the harm?

She caught a glimpse of herself in the mirror—a girl she hardly recognised in the smart, unfamiliar clothes, her eyes unnaturally bright and her cheeks flushed.

And knew exactly why she wouldn't take the risk.

She wrote steadily for the rest of the day, her unaccustomed finery restored to its carrier bags and stowed at the back of the wardrobe. Out of sight, out of mind, she told herself.

And when eventually she ventured out to heat a tin of soup and make a sandwich, the flat was deserted.

She'd just cleared away her makeshift meal when the buzzer sounded. What now? she wondered, groaning silently as she obeyed its summons. Don't tell me Veronica's come back to say all the hotels are full.

But when she opened the door, she found Justin smiling at her.

'Hi,' he said, too casually. 'Is Mark around?'

'No,' she said, her own lips twitching reluctantly. 'But I suspect you knew that already.'

'So, are you going to let me in? I promise I'm safe and house-trained.'

'Also difficult to keep away.' Tallie stood aside to admit him and led the way to the sitting room. 'The choice is tea or coffee. The alcohol belongs to Mark.'

Justin opened the briefcase he was carrying and produced a

bottle. 'Cloudy Bay,' he said. 'Taste it and fall in love. But only with the wine, naturally.'

'Naturally,' Tallie agreed dryly, and went to fetch the corkscrew.

Although unexpected, it was a relaxed and convivial interlude, taking away the sour taste of Veronica Melrose's visit. They talked about books, comparing favourite authors, found they had broadly similar tastes in music, but differed widely on films. And the wine was wonderful.

By the time he left an hour later, she found she'd agreed to accompany him to the theatre the following week, and when he paused at the front door, cupping her chin gently in his hand and bending towards her, she allowed his kiss, which was brief, undemanding, yet undeniably pleasant.

Alone, Tallie smiled as she re-corked what was left of the wine, preparatory to putting it in the fridge, and began to wash the glasses.

There was no denying that Justin was an extremely attractive man. And, with his fair hair and blue eyes, exactly her type, as well as being practically a template for William in her book.

I based him originally on Gareth, she thought. And when Gareth turned out to be not the person I'd hoped, I think I may have stopped believing in William too, and that's why I'm having all these problems in bringing him to life. But maybe it will be easier to put him centre stage from now on.

As for Hugo Cantrell, who was becoming almost too real, and who might have to be killed off in some unpleasant way…

'You look very fierce,' Mark commented from the doorway. 'Is something wrong?'

She almost dropped the glass she was drying. 'I—I didn't hear you come in.'

'Evidently. You were lost in thought.' He looked at the wine bottle on the counter top. 'Been entertaining?'

'Yes, as it happens.' Her tone was defensive.

'May I guess the identity of your visitor?' The note of amusement in his voice was not lost on her.

She stared at him. 'Did you tell him to come?'

'As if.' He leaned a shoulder against the door frame. 'So where's he taking you?'

'To the new Leigh Hanford play,' she admitted unwillingly.

'It's had good reviews,' he said casually. 'He's lucky to get tickets.'

She frowned. 'Did you have anything to do with that?'

'Why, Miss Paget,' he drawled, 'what a suspicious mind you have. I suppose it comes from working out plots.'

'Probably,' she said. 'And now I must go and work out some more of them. Goodnight, Mr Benedict.'

'Goodnight to you, Miss Paget.' He added softly, 'I hope your dreams are sweet.'

Tallie hoped so too as she headed towards her room, but they would have to be delayed. First she would have to find some way of dealing with Hugo Cantrell. After all, the wretched man seemed to be taking over the book, and that was the last thing she wanted. So he would have to go. Painfully and permanently.

At the same time it occurred to her that, although she might be able to remove him from the manuscript, it would not be so easy to erase his dark-haired, green-eyed image from her mind.

Not when she was living with the real thing.

A disturbing reflection that pursued her for the remainder of the night, so that the dreams that eventually punctuated her sleep were restless and uneasy.

CHAPTER EIGHT

'So,' LORNA said eagerly, 'tell me what he's like.'

'Arrogant,' Tallie said coldly. 'Serial womaniser. Fortunately, I don't have to see much of him.'

Lorna gaped at her. 'Then why are you taking all this trouble, if he's so frightful?'

'Oh—' Tallie flushed '—you're talking about Justin.'

And I should be too, she told herself. Talking about him, thinking about, dreaming about him. And not sparing Mark Benedict a second thought.

Especially when he's barely addressed two consecutive sentences to me since his stepmother's visit three weeks ago. He said he owed me, she thought. Yet now he seems to have cut me off completely. Iced me quite deliberately.

'Damn right I'm talking about Justin,' said Lorna.

'Well…' Tallie considered '…he's…lovely. Just as nice as I thought, and I'm having dinner with him tomorrow night at Pierre Martin.'

'Very smart,' her friend approved. 'Also expensive. And you need me to help along the good work by lending you something to wear.' She waved at the open door of her wardrobe. 'Take your pick.'

'I just don't know,' Tallie said, peering wildly along the rail. 'You choose for me.'

'Hmm.' Lorna gave her a shrewd once-over. 'Do you want "Touch me not" or "Come and get me"?'

Tallie blushed more deeply. 'Maybe somewhere in between,' she hedged.

'Wimp,' Lorna said, not unkindly. She paused. 'Tallie, you're not nervous about this dinner date, are you?'

'I think I could be,' Tallie admitted. 'Up to now, it's all been pretty low-key, but I have a feeling that's going to change. And I don't know what to expect.' She sighed. 'Or what he'll expect either.'

'Well, being a man, he'll undoubtedly be hoping,' Lorna returned dryly. 'Especially after dinner and a bottle of wine at Pierre Martin has cost him an arm and a leg. Presumably, he's attractive.'

'Very,' Tallie said emphatically.

'And you trust him?'

'Absolutely.'

'Then what are you waiting for?' Lorna demanded robustly. 'Just—go with the flow.'

She took a dark red dress from the wardrobe and Tallie's eyes widened. 'That's fabulous.'

'It's a good simple style, not too low-cut, not too short.' Lorna held it against her to demonstrate. 'And the colour should be good for you as well. Stop you looking like your own ghost.'

She rummaged in the bottom of the wardrobe. 'And there are shoes to match, plain and not too high. You don't want to risk taking a nosedive, or spraining your ankle.'

That, Tallie thought, could be the least of my problems.

She wasn't sure why she felt so edgy, she thought, as she got ready for her date the following evening. Up to now, she'd enjoyed the moments she'd spent in Justin's arms, for heaven's sake, and she was sure he was far too decent a man to apply undue pressure, or push her into something she wasn't ready for.

But he'd been letting her go with more and more reluctance. Which seemed to indicate that he now wanted their relationship to be more than just friendly. And maybe she should stop worrying and regard the night ahead as simply a step on the way to falling in love with a man she liked.

But with some bruises of his own.

Or that was what Mark Benedict had said, anyway. And if they'd still been having even some rudimentary form of conversation, she might have asked him what he'd meant. But she wasn't risking another snub, as he stalked past her on the way to heaven knew where.

Clearly, she thought, he didn't like being in her debt, and regretted the impulse that had caused him to ask for her help. And any hint at a new understanding between them had relapsed once more into the silence of that first week. A silence she didn't know how to break, and which was clearly intended to keep her at a distance.

Which was how matters between them still stood, and she'd probably been a fool to expect anything different.

'Same roof—separate lives.' That was what he'd said, and what he meant.

But the situation was less embarrassing than she'd feared, because most of the time he wasn't around. He'd been off to Germany, Canada for three days, and Venezuela for four, and in between he'd been fitting in meetings all over Britain.

'Doesn't he ever slow down?' she'd asked Penny, who'd turned up quite unexpectedly one evening during one of his longer absences, bringing a Chinese take-away—on the off-chance, she said cheerfully, that Tallie hadn't eaten yet.

'I only wish he would.' Penny sighed. 'He's got a terrific team working for him, and he could delegate far more. For instance, there was no need for him to be caught up in that hideous African mess, but he knew there was trouble brewing and he didn't want to risk anyone who had a wife and family.'

'And now he's going back there,' Tallie said, half to herself.

'He has a job to finish.' Penny shrugged fatalistically. 'That's the way he is.'

And they'd turned to other topics.

Tallie had enjoyed seeing Penny again, but had backed off when further meetings were suggested. However, it wasn't simply the lack of time or money that she'd used as her excuse, and which

Penny had reluctantly accepted, which had made her demur, but more the suspicion that Mark might not approve of any burgeoning friendship between her and his cousin.

That it might impinge on his 'separate lives' ruling.

But I wish I'd asked her about Justin, she thought. Except that it might have revived unhappy memories about her own bruises.

She zipped herself into her dress, wondering doubtfully if it had been stupid to spend money on a new broderie anglais bra and briefs set from her favourite chain store.

But if—something was going to happen tonight, she would need all the confidence going, and some pretty lingerie could only boost her self-esteem.

She was on her way down the passage to the front door when Mark emerged from the study, stretching wearily. He paused, his gaze travelling over her, taking in the demure charm of the red dress with narrow-eyed speculation.

'Ah,' he said softly. 'Big date tonight.'

An almost civil remark, thought Tallie furiously, and just when it was needed least. How very typical. And if she'd left five minutes earlier, she could have avoided him altogether.

She lifted her chin, saying coolly, 'I am going out, yes.' And tried to ignore how his glance seemed to be lingering on the way the dress clung to her small high breasts and the slender curve of her hips.

'Then clearly I won't bother to wait up,' he murmured and sauntered off in the direction of the kitchen.

And Tallie made her escape, thankful he hadn't hung around to watch her blushing.

Justin was already at the restaurant, and he stood, taking her hand and kissing her on the cheek as she joined him at their table.

'You look lovely.' His eyes were warm with admiration, and possibly more. 'Is that a new dress?'

New to me anyway, she thought, basking in his appreciation. It will be all right, she told herself. Everything will be fine.

She looked about her with interest as she took her seat beside him on the cushioned bench against the wall. Most of the tables were occupied, and waiters moved between them with quiet efficiency. There was no canned music, just the hum of contented conversation, punctuated by the occasional pop of a cork.

She sat back with a sigh. 'What a nice place this is.'

'I came to the opening about a year ago,' he said after a brief hesitation. 'So I know the food is good.' His mouth quirked. 'After the meal you cooked for us that night, I felt nothing less would do.'

Tallie laughed, and after that everything became easier. It was fun to sit close to him and chat over a shared menu, which was short but crammed with delicious possibilities. Rather like the evening itself, she thought with sudden shyness.

Because Justin's gentle flirting had a new and definite purpose since their last encounter, and it was exciting to realise that, for the first time in her life, she was being seriously propositioned.

She recognised, too, that before long she would need to make a decision, and therefore it would be better not to drink too much of the wonderful wine he'd picked to accompany the food, in case it clouded her judgement.

Or had her choice really been made from the moment she'd accepted tonight's invitation? She couldn't be sure.

For dessert, Justin ordered two of the restaurant's famous chocolate soufflés.

'And coffee, *m'sieur*?'

'I think we'll decide that later.' Looking at Tallie, he added softly, 'Shall we?'

The moment had arrived. He was asking if she'd go back with him to his flat and he required an answer, she thought numbly, staring down at the white linen tablecloth. She could say yes or no. Nod or shake her head. Anything rather than sit as if she'd been turned to stone, her heart the only part of her body that seemed to be working, as it pounded unevenly away against her ribcage. As she tried desperately to *think*…

She was aware of the waiter moving away, but only realised someone else had taken his place when he spoke.

'Good God, Justin. You're the last person I expected to see here.'

Tallie glanced up, startled by the challenge implicit in the harsh drawl.

The newcomer was a youngish man, with a round, pug-like face, unbecomingly flushed as he stood over them.

'This is a restaurant, Clive, and we all have to eat,' Justin returned coolly. 'Even you,' he added, with a fleeting glance at their visitor's overweight body snugly encased in its dark blue suit. 'Please don't let us keep you.'

'Oh, I'm over there.' He waved a vague hand. 'Family party. They couldn't believe their eyes either, so I came across to check.'

He paused. 'Life treating you well, is it? Job…all tickety-boo and no regrets? You certainly seem to be recovering in other ways.'

Tallie found herself the unwelcome target of small, leering brown eyes. 'Although, to be honest, she's a little young for you, isn't she, old boy? Bit fresh from the makers? I didn't know you were into cradle-snatching.'

Justin beckoned to the nearest waiter. He said quietly, 'I think Mr Nelson wishes to rejoin his friends. And cancel the soufflés, please. We'll just have coffee.'

'Oh, don't run away on my account. Okay, sunshine, I'm going.' This to the waiter, before he turned back to Justin. 'Always a pleasure to see you, old man. And good luck to you, poppet.'

When he'd gone there was a long silence.

Justin didn't look at her. 'Tallie, I must apologise for that.' His voice sounded odd, as if it were coming from some other, far-distant world. 'I…I don't know what to say. But I think… maybe…it would be better if I just…got the bill and found you a cab.'

He added, his face bleak with embarrassment, 'I wish I knew how to explain, but I can't. You see, I—I just didn't realise…'

How young I am?

But you must have done, she argued silently as his voice tailed away. You had to know when you met me—the first time you took me out—that I wasn't very old, or very experienced. Yet you asked to see me again. You let me think it didn't matter…

She swallowed past the tightness in her throat. It hardly seemed possible this was happening to her again. That he was rejecting her as Gareth had done, and for the same reason. When, only a few minutes before, it had seemed she would be the one to choose how the evening should end.

He couldn't have wanted her very much, she thought, if he was allowing some snide comments from some passing half-drunk acquaintance to tip the balance against her. To prompt him to take another long look, and realise he was making a big mistake.

So maybe it was for the best, and she should even be grateful to the obnoxious Clive for intervening before she'd had a chance to commit herself, thus saving her from the possibility of even worse embarrassment later.

But I won't think about that now, she told herself with determination. I'll just concentrate on getting out of here with a little dignity. I can do that. I've had previous practice.

She lifted her chin, forcing herself to smile.

'Heavens, there's nothing to explain.' She kept her tone bright and friendly. 'It's getting late, and we both have to work tomorrow. I—I've had a lovely evening, and you were absolutely right about the food. It's amazing.'

She kept up a flow of chatter until they were outside, and a passing cab drew up obediently beside them in response to Justin's signal.

'But there's really no need for you to come with me,' she told him as he gave the address to the driver. 'I'll be fine.'

'If that's what you want.' He looked at her, his face troubled, as he handed the driver the money for the fare, then paused. 'Tallie—I'll call you.'

'Well—that would have been nice,' she said, still smiling. 'But I'm afraid I'm not going to have much free time for a while. It's been terrific, but I have rather been neglecting my book. But—thanks, anyway.'

And she shot into the back of the cab, closing the door smartly behind her, just in case he was contemplating kissing her goodnight, as some sort of consolation prize. Even sent him a cheery wave as the vehicle moved off.

Before slumping back, shivering, into the corner.

All that inner heart-searching, said a jeering voice in her head. All that panic-stricken debate about whether he was the right man, and if you were doing the right thing. All for nothing.

She bit her lip. In fact, totally wasted on someone who'd suddenly decided, when push came to shove, that she didn't suit his requirements after all, even if he wasn't as overtly brutal about it as Gareth had been.

But she still felt stranded, and very foolish, her fragile confidence in herself yet again torn to ribbons.

In the end, the red dress hadn't helped at all. It had just been another error of judgement, along with the new underwear, she thought, flinching.

And when she returned it, Lorna, of course, would be eager to know how the evening had gone, although a simple, 'I didn't fancy him enough after all,' would probably deal with that particular problem.

She trailed slowly up to the flat, letting herself in quietly and with deliberate care, just wanting to reach the sanctuary of her room.

But her luck was still out because, as she closed the door, Mark's voice said sharply from the sitting room, 'Tallie, is that you?' And next moment he appeared in the doorway, staring at her, his brows drawn together.

'Back already?' He checked his watch, then glanced past her. 'So, where's Justin?'

'Well, I'm not hiding him in my handbag.' She managed a degree of insouciance. 'He went home. Isn't that what most people do at the end of the evening?'

He was still frowning. 'But I thought…'

'Did you? And so did I for a while. But we were both wrong.'

'Evidently.' He paused, then said almost abruptly, 'I've only just got back myself. I've opened a bottle of wine. Would you like to share some with me?'

She hesitated, surprised. After his recent aloofness, she'd hardly expected any kind of friendly overture from him. Or did he just feel sorry for her because she'd obviously been dumped?

Instinct told her to make a polite excuse and escape into her room, to nurse her wounded feelings and damaged pride in private. On the other hand, did she really want to be on her own? And, besides, she'd spent a relatively abstemious evening and some alcohol might help her sleep.

She tried to smile. 'I thought it was supposed to be tea and sympathy.'

'Who mentioned sympathy?' He motioned her past him into the sitting room. 'I'll get a glass for you.'

The room was softly lit by a single lamp. The wine, a St Emilion, was standing open on the coffee table, his half-filled glass beside it.

Tallie kicked off her shoes and curled up on the sofa opposite, her feet tucked under her. When he returned, she accepted the glass he handed her with a murmur of thanks.

'However, a toast hardly seems appropriate under the circumstances,' he remarked, resuming his seat, lounging against the cushions. He was barefoot too, she noticed, and casual in a dark blue V-necked sweater over his close-fitting jeans. Then, afraid he might notice that she was looking at him, she hastily transferred her attention to the glowing ruby in her glass.

'Probably not,' she agreed stiltedly. 'Did…did you have a pleasant evening?'

'I went to the cinema,' he said, 'to see a film so enthralling that I came out halfway through it, deciding that life was too short to remain any longer.' He shrugged a shoulder. 'But maybe I wasn't in the mood.'

'You went alone?'

'Well, don't sound so surprised,' Mark returned. 'I do spend the occasional few hours in my own company.'

'I just thought you'd have gone with Miss Randall.'

He said dryly, 'Sonia only likes films where you need subtitles to understand the subtitles. Tonight's effort was rather more basic. Now is there anything else you want to know about my relationship with Miss Randall, or can we file the whole subject under "Forget It"?'

'Willingly,' Tallie said shortly, and drank some of her wine.

'And don't sulk,' he added.

She was forming a dignified denial of any such intention, when the sheer absurdity of it struck her and her mouth twisted into a reluctant smile.

'That's better,' he said. 'So, now we've discussed my disappointing evening, let's talk about yours. Did you and Justin have a row?'

She shook her head. 'No, nothing like that. We had a marvellous dinner, then he decided, as he had every right to do, that I wasn't old enough or sufficiently sophisticated for him. End of story.'

'I can't honestly believe that.' He was frowning again. 'Are you sure there wasn't some kind of misunderstanding?'

'I'm certain,' she said. 'I think "cradle-snatching" is frank enough to remove any lingering doubt. Don't you?'

'Cradle-snatching?' he repeated slowly. 'But that's ludicrous, bordering on crazy. Because you, Natalie Paget, are not a child by any stretch of the imagination.' He paused, then added quietly, 'And when you look as you do tonight, I'd have said you were irresistible.'

Startled colour invaded her face and she felt her breathing quicken. The silence that followed his words seemed to be growing, thickening in some inexplicable and disturbing way, and it needed to be broken.

She said hurriedly, 'But clearly Justin is aware of…of the age difference between us, and it…worries him.'

'Age difference,' he echoed derisively. 'God in heaven, the poor bastard's thirty, a year younger than I am. Neither of us is looking forward to drawing his pension quite yet.'

'I didn't mean that.'

'I'm relieved to hear it.' His voice held a touch of grimness as he refilled his glass.

'Because my lack of…worldly wisdom is probably a more important issue.'

'My God,' he said. 'If this is how the debate went, I'm not surprised the evening ended early.'

'There was no debate,' she said. 'I'm just trying to make some sense of it all.'

He said slowly, 'Maybe it just wasn't meant to be. Consider that.'

'I could,' she said. 'I would. Only this isn't the first time it's happened. As I once mentioned.'

'I hadn't forgotten.'

She forced a smile. 'Yes—well, I'm beginning to feel as if I have two heads.'

'Not from this angle. And, as I think I also once mentioned, maybe you should consider your innocence a bonus rather than a burden.'

She said in a low voice, 'But it isn't as easy as that. I feel like a total anomaly—a freak in a world where girls, years younger than me, have forgotten more about sex than I'll ever know.'

He contemplated his wine. 'You consider that a good thing?'

'Not particularly. Just—the way it is. And for some reason, I'm out of the loop.'

'Maybe that isn't a bad place to be,' he said. 'There are far worse, believe me. And now I think it's time you went to bed.'

She stared at him, a few feet away from her in the lamplight, taking in the incisive lines of nose, the firmly sculpted mouth and the cool brilliance of his eyes. Allowing the imprint of the long, lean body with its broad shoulders and narrow hips to burn into her mind. Really—looking at him in a way she hadn't done before, as a thought was born. And became a resolve.

She said in a voice she didn't recognise, 'Will you come with me?'

His head lifted sharply and for a moment he was utterly still, looking back at her in silence.

Then he got to his feet, walked across and took the glass from her hand. He said quite gently, 'You've probably had more than enough to drink. So I'll pretend you didn't say that.'

She stared up at him. 'Mark, I'm not drunk. Not on two glasses of wine over the entire evening, for heaven's sake. I'm just someone who's sick of being thought of—dismissed as a child. And I'm asking…you to help me become a woman.'

'Offering yourself to the nearest man is hardly a sign of maturity,' he returned curtly. 'And, anyway, what you ask is impossible.'

'Because of your "same roof—separate lives" ruling?' As he turned away, she caught at his hand, halting him. 'But that needn't change because…because of anything that happens tonight. It will begin and end here, and afterwards things will go back to exactly the way they were between us. I swear it.'

She swallowed. 'I just want to lose my virginity, not embark on any kind of relationship.'

'Dear God, Tallie, that's exactly what you should want,' he said harshly, releasing his fingers from her clasp. 'Just be patient. Things may not have worked out with Justin for some reason, but you'll meet someone else—someone you'll fall in love with, and you'll be glad you…waited for him.'

'But if and when I meet this man, it has to be on equal terms,' she said vehemently. 'No hang-ups or feelings of inadequacy because I'm embarking on unknown territory.'

'Unknown?' he repeated. 'How can it possibly be that, when films and television make it graphically clear what goes on? But if you're still in any doubt, buy a good sex manual.'

'I don't mean—the mechanics of it, but how it relates to me. How I'm going to feel while it's happening. For all I know, I could be frigid.'

'Doubtful,' he said. 'In the extreme.'

'But I need to be sure.' She took a gulp of wine and set down the glass. 'Also there's far more chance of it being…good with him—the man I love—once the…the first time has been dealt with. You must see that.'

He'd resumed his seat opposite. 'I'm not sure that I do.'

She bit her lip. 'Well, I know—at least I've been told—that sex is usually pretty much of a disaster to begin with—painful, messy and even downright embarrassing. So I'd like…all that to be over and done with before I really…make love with someone who actually matters to me.'

'Ah,' he said. 'And just how have I come to feature in this unappealing scenario?'

She lifted her chin. 'Because you owe me,' she said bluntly. 'You said so.'

'Yes,' he said slowly. 'But this is not the kind of recompense I had in mind.'

'And also because we…we don't care about each other,' she went on. 'You said that too—that we have nothing going for us but an uneasy truce. So it won't actually matter if it turns out to be…' She hesitated.

'A catastrophe of epic proportions,' he suggested.

She gave him a suspicious glance. 'Are you laughing at me?'

'No,' he said. 'I've never been further from amusement in my life.' He got up and walked to the window, pulling back the curtain to stare into the darkness. 'You're making me see myself in a whole new light, sweetheart,' he tossed back over his shoulder. 'The unfeeling bastard who walks away, leaving innocent girls crushed and bleeding.'

'I never thought that for a minute.' She bit her lip. 'Oh God, I've said this all wrong, haven't I? I just wanted you to know that, if you agreed, I'd have no expectations afterwards—wouldn't make any waves. You'd have nothing to worry about on that score. We'll just…resume the truce, until I can find somewhere else to live and get out of your life for good. Which was always the plan, anyway.'

She paused. 'As for…for the rest of it, I assumed you'd know…what you were doing. That you'd probably try not to hurt me. After all, you've had enough experience…' She stopped with a gasp, realising this remark was hardly felicitous either.

'Women by the cartload,' Mark agreed expressionlessly, his back still turned to her. 'But, unfortunately, it's not Tuesday, which is my usual day for deflowering virgins.'

She said quietly, 'Now you are making fun of me.'

'Yes—no. Hell, I'm not even sure any more.' He swung back to look at her, pushing a hand through his hair. 'For God's sake, Tallie, let's forget this grotesque conversation ever began. You don't know what you're asking.'

'Would it really be such a hardship?' She got to her feet. 'Earlier, you said I was…irresistible. But that's not true, is it, Mark? Because you don't seem to have any problem in resisting me. So why say it, if you didn't mean it?'

'Because at the time I wasn't fighting some latent sense of decency, damn you.' His voice was harsh, goaded. 'But perhaps I should give up the battle.' He paused. 'Turn round—slowly.'

Bewildered, she obeyed him, her skirt brushing against her legs as she performed a complete circle. Aware, as she did so, of a faint, disturbing smile playing round his mouth as he watched her.

He said softly, 'Now, take off your clothes and do that again—even more slowly. Just to refresh my memory.'

She stared back at him, her lips parting in shock, and saw his smile widen.

'Losing your nerve, sweetheart?' he gibed. 'Wondering if you really want to be naked in front of me again? Especially when you know this time I'm going to do a damned sight more than just look.'

Tallie swallowed. She said, 'If it's…what you want…' And fumbled for the zip at the back of her dress.

'No,' he said sharply, halting her. 'It isn't—merely a final attempt to bring you to your senses, which doesn't appear to be working. Therefore…'

He walked over to her, pushing a tumbled strand of hair back from her face, his thumb lingering almost ruefully on her cheekbone before tracing the curve of her face and the line of her jaw.

It was the lightest of touches but somehow it seemed to burn through flesh and bone and down into the very core of her, and Tallie found herself swallowing back a gasp.

He said quietly, 'This is a new situation for me, so maybe you should just go along to your room and I'll join you there presently. When I've had a chance to think a little.'

She nodded. Tried to smile. Failed. And slipped away—to wait.

And waiting, she realised, as she sat rigidly on the edge of the bed, might well turn out to be the worst part of it all. This tense anticipation of the moment when the door would open and he would come to her. When she would finally…know, and be known.

Because, hopefully—mercifully—*that* would probably be over quite quickly.

In the meantime, the uncertainty was getting to her. What should she do? Undress—lie down on the bed? Like some maiden sacrifice on a pagan altar, she thought, crushing down the bubble of appalled hysteria rising in her throat.

Only it wasn't like that at all. Just a calculated, clinical solution to a problem. Or would be, when it happened.

She got up and began to pace restlessly round the room, rear-ranging things on the dressing table. Closing the lid of the laptop. Picking up the clean skirt draped over the back of the chair and hanging it in the wardrobe.

Somehow it was essential to have the room totally neat and tidy, she thought, even if she herself was in turmoil.

She stared at the door. Oh, where was he? Why was he taking so long? Or had she simply misheard him? Did he want her to go to his room instead? Perhaps that was it.

Well, there was only one way to find out.

She walked quietly up the passage, past the silent office, the deserted sitting room and the darkened kitchen. His door was ajar and she knocked quietly at first, then more firmly.

'Mark.' She swallowed. 'Mark, are you there?'

But the room was empty, the bed unruffled. No shower running in the adjoining bathroom either.

In fact, no sound in the entire flat. She looked around, feeling suddenly very cold as she realised that he'd gone. That he'd walked away, leaving her quite alone.

Realised, too, as pain gripped her, that this was the worst rejection of them all, because it was one that she'd brought entirely on herself. And that, somehow, she would have to deal with the shame of that as well.

If I can, she thought, without breaking into a thousand pieces. And turned away.

CHAPTER NINE

THE shoes she'd discarded earlier were still on the sitting room floor. Tallie picked them up and sank down on the sofa, gripping them tightly. Pretty shoes, she thought. And a pretty colour. She remembered admiring them as she had dressed that evening. While she'd been getting ready for the important dinner date that she'd thought she would remember always.

And so she would, but not for any of the reasons she'd expected.

And now she'd made everything a hundred times worse by throwing herself at yet another man who didn't want her. At Mark Benedict, of all people in the entire world.

A chance to think. That was what he'd said. And he'd gone away and thought, and obviously decided it was impossible. That he couldn't go through with it.

But why hadn't he told her so? Tallie wondered numbly. Did he really think he was letting her down lightly by—vanishing without even an attempt at explanation?

Yet what could he really have said?

And what on earth could she say, or do, when she saw him again? She'd have to think of something—another salvage job. Maybe she should apologise, be contrite, even a little sheepish as she admitted that the whole thing had been madness. That she was nothing but a child, after all, hell-bent on making a fool of herself. And she was only glad he'd recognised that in time to stop her careering blindly into the mistake of a lifetime.

And, if she was really lucky, he might even believe her.

She shuddered. I'd like to run too, she thought. But where can I go—and at this hour?

The wine he'd taken from her was on the table. She let the shoes fall back on the carpet and reached for the glass instead. She would drink the contents and follow them with whatever was left in the bottle. She hoped wearily that there'd be enough to get her drunk, or at least impose some kind of oblivion so that she would stop hurting so much.

It was the memory of pleading with him, she thought. The searing, scarring knowledge that she'd begged him to take her that somehow made all this so much worse than anything that had gone before.

That was the only explanation for the icy pain that was consuming her. Making her want to bury her face in the cushions and weep.

But she must never let him know it. Never give a sign that his decision had caused her even the slightest pang. It was essential that he should think it was simply guilt and embarrassment that would be keeping her so determinedly out of his way while she stayed under his roof.

And that could not be for much longer, whatever the cost. Because she knew now that the price she would pay if she stayed would be even higher.

In the stillness, the slam of the front door brought her unhappy reverie to an abrupt end. Tallie's hand jerked, spilling a few drops of wine on her dress as she turned in disbelief to see Mark stride into the room.

'Tallie?' He halted, brows lifting sardonically. 'Not cowering under the bedclothes, waiting for me to blight your girlhood? I'm surprised.'

She said, 'I—I thought you'd changed your mind.'

'Far from it,' he said. 'I went to find an all-night chemist.'

'Oh,' she said, biting her lip as light belatedly dawned.

'Oh, indeed,' he echoed with faint mockery. 'Poor Tallie, is safe sex a little too much reality for you?'

'No.' She lifted her chin, a mass of conflicting emotions at war inside her. 'I was hardly expecting romance. I'm not that stupid.'

He came across to her. Removed the glass from her hand again. 'Anaesthetic?' he asked and shook his head. 'You don't want your senses dulled, sweetheart, and I certainly don't. I need you completely awake and totally aware.'

He took her hands and drew her to her feet. 'Now come with me.'

If ever there was a moment to tell him that she'd had second thoughts herself and he was off the hook, it had to be now.

And yet, somehow, she was being led unresistingly by him down the passage to her bedroom and he was shutting the door, closing them in together in the softness of the single bedside lamp.

Tallie stood there, hands at her sides, watching as he removed his jacket, then extracted a packet from his jeans and put it on the night table.

It was all so—practical, even casual, she thought, swallowing, and maybe she should try to be equally matter-of-fact. Especially as he was here by her invitation.

He pulled his sweater over his head and discarded it and, as his hands went to the waistband of his jeans, Tallie turned away, reaching for the zip on her dress, struggling unsuccessfully to tug it down. Telling herself, as she'd done earlier, that undressing in front of him didn't matter because he already knew what she looked like naked. Except now it wouldn't stop at looking: He'd told her so and, now the moment had come, the prospect of what lay ahead of her was drying her mouth and making her fingers clumsy.

'Having problems?'

Too many, and all of my own making. Aloud, she said huskily, 'I—I think there's some material caught in it.'

His voice was quite gentle. 'Come here.'

She went to him slowly, observing with a kind of relief that he was still wearing his jeans. 'I feel so stupid.'

'Why should you?' he asked. 'After all, I shall enjoy undressing you, darling, far more than you seem to be doing.' He added with faint amusement, 'Or do you intend me to share your lack of pleasure in what's about to happen? If so, I can guarantee you'll be disappointed, because I plan to savour every minute.'

She tried to think of something to say, some clever answer, but her mind seemed suddenly blank and it was easier to stand in silence under his hands.

Deftly, he released the scrap of fabric and undid the zip to its full extent. Then he slipped the dress from her shoulders, allowing it to slide easily down her body to the floor.

Tallie waited, head bent, during the endless pause as he looked at her, clad in nothing but those two pretty scraps of broderie anglaise. Then he said quietly, 'Just seeing you like this, Tallie, makes it all worthwhile.'

And, taking her rigid body in his arms, he kissed her.

His mouth was warm as it moved on hers, and gentle in a way she had not anticipated.

After all, he'd not set out to seduce her. Apart from that first hideous encounter in his shower, he'd never by word or gesture indicated even a fleeting desire for her. And while there'd been brief moments that approached understanding between them, there'd been no tenderness.

He didn't want to be here in any real sense, so she'd expected him to demand rather than ask, and to take rather than seek, wasting no time on any kind of wooing.

And that was fine, she told herself, because she, too, wanted the entire process over and done with quickly, her body and her bed all her own again. Their uneasy truce restored.

Which was why she found the deliberate restraint of this first caress faintly disturbing. But if he was playing some private waiting game, hoping for a response, he could think again, because it wasn't going to happen.

So she stood passive in his embrace, her lips unyielding to his delicate pressure.

He was holding her lightly too, his fingertips merely brushing her skin as they stroked its cool and silken texture and began an initial exploration of the planes and curves of her slenderness. Making her aware of an unwelcome answering quiver along her nerve-endings that she had never experienced before. A confusing reaction which made her heart pound unevenly and set her suddenly racing towards panic.

She pulled away from him. She said huskily, 'You don't have to treat me as if I'm made of glass. I—I know why we're here.'

He looked at her for a long moment, the green eyes narrowing. 'You prefer the more direct approach. Fine.' He picked her up and threw her across the bed, following her down and kneeling over her. He unzipped his jeans with one hand, then hooked two fingers into the fragile band of Tallie's briefs with unmistakable and deliberate purpose.

'No.' Her hands lifted, pushing at him frantically, her voice hoarse. 'You can't—not like this—oh, God, please…'

'I could,' he returned grimly. 'And I'd enjoy it and persuade you to do the same—under the right circumstances. But not, I admit, for your first time.'

He lifted himself away from her, lying beside her in silence. Eventually he sighed and turned back to her, his hand sliding under the soft fall of her hair to cup the nape of her neck, his touch sending another immediate *frisson* rippling down her spine.

He said quietly, 'Tallie—you told me you wanted this.'

'I did.' She didn't look at him as her breathing quickened. 'I do. It's just…'

'Then please accept that we're batting on the same side here, and try to trust me.' He paused. 'Now, I'm going to finish undressing and get into bed. If you really intend to continue, I suggest you do the same.'

He swung himself to the edge of the bed, turning his back to her, while Tallie wriggled to the opposite edge and sat there for a moment, trying to steady herself.

And recover my nerve as well, she thought wryly. Up to now, I've behaved like a complete idiot, and it would serve me right if he'd walked out on me. But he seems prepared to stay if I—I…

Behind her, she was aware of movement, the soft creak of the mattress. And his voice saying, 'I'm waiting.'

She allowed herself no more hesitation. After all, she was here for a purpose which was about to be fulfilled, so she simply unhooked her bra, dropping it to the floor, then sent her briefs to follow it before she slid hurriedly under the covers, lying on her back, her arms at her sides and staring up at the ceiling.

Mark propped himself on an elbow, looking down at her. He said, a ghost of laughter in his voice, 'I get an overwhelming impression of teeth being gritted. I know it's what made England great, but it doesn't work quite so well in bed.'

He added more gently, 'And, in spite of anything I've said, Tallie, if you decide at any time that you want me to stop, you only have to tell me.' He paused. 'From my personal point of view, I'd prefer it to be sooner rather than later. And definitely well before the point of no return. I don't want to ache for a week.'

She said in a low voice, 'I—I won't ask you to stop. You're being very patient with me. I know that and I'm—grateful.'

'I can be more patient than you've ever dreamed,' he told her quietly. 'And I'm hoping for a damned sight more than gratitude.'

He smoothed her hair back from her face. 'Now, stop fighting me, my sweet, and start listening to what your body's already begun to tell you. Will you do that?'

'I'll—try. I really will—Mark.' She pronounced his name carefully, as she turned towards him, lifting a hand, shyly, tentatively to rest on his bare shoulder, feeling the muscles flex under her hesitant touch.

And as he bent towards her, she raised her mouth to his.

This time his kiss was harder, as he explored the softness of her mouth, then probed more intimately, the silken invasion of his tongue allowing him to taste all the inner honeyed sweetness that he sought, and draw from her a first diffident response.

With a murmur of satisfaction against her lips, he gathered her closer, so that her body touched all the warm, lean nakedness of his, her breasts grazed by the roughness of his chest hair, his hands splayed across her back.

When at last he raised his head, they were both breathless. Mark glanced down to where the concealing sheet had fallen away, baring her rose-tipped breasts to his gaze.

He said softly, 'Exquisite.'

She flushed, turning her head away. 'They're too small.' Her voice was husky.

'No,' he said. 'They're utterly adorable. Because I can do this.' He cupped one soft mound in his palm, stroking the nipple gently with his thumb, watching as it puckered and hardened into throbbing life. 'And also this,' he added softly, taking the pink, aching peak between his lips and teasing it with his tongue.

Sensation pierced her, a glancing pleasure shockingly akin to pain, as it arrowed its path through bone and blood to the secret centre of her womanhood, and Tallie heard herself make a small bewildered sound that was almost a moan.

His mouth returned to hers, lingering there, while his fingers continued their delicate erotic teasing of her breasts, arousing them to an intensity of need that was almost anguish.

Tallie found she was reaching for him in turn, her hands gliding over his shoulders, learning the strong line of his throat, and the hollows at its base. Pressing her palms against the flat male nipples and feeling the vibrant power of his heartbeat. Aware too of the potent male hardness pressing against her thighs, and not knowing whether to be scared or exultant over this undeniable proof that he wanted her.

He was questing further now as he caressed her, taking all the time in the world and making her whole body tremble under the subtle play of his lean hands. And where his fingers touched, his lips followed, delineating the blue tracery of veins in wrists and arms, and the delicate structure of collar-bone and ribcage, then marking the indentation of her slim waist and the slight concavity of her belly. Whispering soft words of pleasure against her skin.

There were tiny sparks dancing behind her closed eyelids. He'd told her to listen to her body, she thought, her mind reeling, and it was telling her with shocking, almost terrifying frankness how much she already—incredibly—wanted him in return.

And when he turned her in his arms so that his mouth could trail tiny kisses down the length of her spine, her body arched in shivering, gasping delight, mutely, blindly seeking more, her breasts swelling into his hands, the nipples aroused to acute tumescence by his touch.

He let his hands move down, gliding over her flanks and the swell of her buttocks, stroking them rhythmically, almost soothingly, except that it was arousal he was offering, not assurance, and her body was already in tumult, her bewildered senses fainting.

Because this was not the soulless learning procedure she'd bargained for and might have dealt with—not this sweating, sticky ferment of sensation, where she was lost, drowning in feelings she hadn't realised could exist. Scared by the sheer force of her own needs.

Mark drew her back against him, his lips caressing the side of her throat, one hand moving to pleasure the taut mounds of her breasts, while the other began a leisurely traverse of her stomach, skimming the hollow of her pelvis to reach, with tantalising slowness, her slender thighs, and linger there, fondling their pliant softness, before sweeping his fingers from her knee to the curve of her hip and back again.

Building on the insidious torment he'd already created, forcing her to writhe in his arms with urgent, impotent need, because he was touching her everywhere but *there*—those soft, hidden places where, to her shame, she most craved him. Where she was burning for him, melting for him, her breath sobbing from her throat as she whispered his name.

At last, just when she thought she would have to beg, his hand moved, cupping the silken triangle at the joining of her thighs for one heart-stopping moment, then drifting inwards, brushing like gossamer over her secret flesh and the tiny sensitive bud it concealed and pausing there to coax it erect, before gliding onwards to let his fingers penetrate the molten core of her with one sure and gentle thrust.

She said, 'Oh, God,' her voice choking, almost extinguished, as she felt her body flood with delight and she lifted herself against him not merely accepting what he'd done, but inciting him deliberately to deepen his exploration of her most intimate being.

Realising at the same time that his thumb had rediscovered that small nub of damp, heated, responsive flesh and was skilfully continuing its arousal, stroking it with a delicate, yet sensual mastery that made it difficult for her to breathe. Driving her, urging her far into that dark and unknown place that she'd feared.

Because Tallie was aware of a feeling growing inside her that transcended excitement, an inexorable spiral of intensity threatening her last remnants of control, and she was close to panic because what was happening to her now was already too much and she couldn't bear any more. Couldn't…

She tried to say, Stop—please stop…but the only sound emerging from the tightness of her throat was a small frantic moan that spelled desire, not protest.

And then it was altogether too late, because she was caught, swept irresistibly away on a rising tide of sensation that was almost an agony. Finding herself lifted to some pinnacle, then flung from it, crying out as her straining, panting body convulsed in spasm after spasm of helpless, exquisite pleasure, before she was sent spinning, back down to a reality that had changed for ever.

And as she lay, limp, wrung out, the only immobile element in a still trembling universe, she became aware that Mark was moving her, placing her gently back against the pillows.

Opening dazed eyes, she found him beside her, leaning on one elbow and watching her—just as he had been, she thought, when it all began, minutes, hours, aeons ago.

She said in a shadow of a voice, 'I thought I was going to die.'

'Yet here you are, alive and incredibly well.' His hand stroked her cheek, then moved lightly down the line of her throat to mould the curve of her shoulder and rest there. 'Maybe your scare-mongering friends should have extended their terms of reference—mentioned the amazing power of the orgasm.'

She said shakily, 'Perhaps they didn't know.'

'That might well be true.' He sounded faintly amused. 'Which puts you ahead on points, my sweet, and definitely not frigid.'

A sudden wave of shyness swept over her. She tried to think of something appropriate to say. In the end, all she could manage was a feeble, 'Thank you.'

He was grinning openly now. 'Happy to have been of service, ma'am.' He paused. 'But it's not all over yet. As you must have realised.'

'Yes—yes, of course.' How could she not, she thought, swallowing, when he was lying close to her, naked, the evidence impossible to ignore? And it seemed they were back to matter-of-fact again. Well, that was fine with her. She said, aiming for casual, 'I—I'm perfectly willing.'

Mark shook his head. 'I don't think so,' he said. 'Not at this precise moment, but soon. And I can wait.'

She could have asked what he meant, but she suspected she already knew because she could feel her skin warming, beginning to tingle under the hand quietly smoothing her shoulder.

Oh, God, she thought, shaken, as realisation dawned. This can't be true. It just isn't happening to me, not again. He can't make me feel like this so soon. It's wrong…

He said softly, 'You're gritting your teeth again, Tallie.' And, drawing her back into his arms, he kissed her. For a moment she tried to resist, but the warm, sensuous movement of his mouth on hers was altogether too shamefully enticing and instead her lips parted, sighing her surrender.

Immediately, his kiss deepened, turning gentleness into passionate, almost ruthless demand, and she twined her arms round his neck, answering him with all her new-found ardour, pressing her body against his in open invitation, and he groaned softly as his hands found her eager breasts, caressing the swollen peaks to throbbing glory.

At last he tore his mouth from hers with open reluctance, moving out of her embrace, and Tallie murmured in breathless protest, reaching for him again.

'Yes, darling.' His own voice was husky, ragged. 'But first I have to take care of you.'

She waited, her body melting for him, longing for his return in a way that left no room for pretence or embarrassment at the realities of desire. And she looked up at him, her eyes widening endlessly, as he moved over her, covering her with his body. He entered her slowly, his gaze searching her face for any sign of discomfort or dissent as, with infinite care, he sheathed the hard strength of his manhood in her yielding woman's flesh.

And for an instant she braced herself, expecting to be hurt, but it didn't happen. Instead of the pain or difficulty she'd believed would be inevitable, however willing she might be, there was only acceptance—and a sense of completion, as if she'd been created for this moment—and this man.

She lifted her hands almost languidly to his shoulders and gripped them, a smile wavering on her lips as she answered the unspoken question in his eyes. He bent his head in silent acknowledgement, then began to move unhurriedly inside her, his long, even thrusts, Tallie soon realised, tempered with deliberate restraint.

She murmured, her breath catching, 'Mark, I told you before—I'm not made of glass, so I don't think you need to be…so patient…any longer.'

He said hoarsely, 'Tallie, I could hurt you.'

'You won't.'

'You don't know…'

'Then show me,' she whispered and, obeying an instinct she hardly understood, she raised her legs, and clasped them round his hips, locking herself to him. 'Show me.'

Mark groaned softly, fiercely, his rhythm altering with stark immediacy, his hard body driving powerfully into hers with a new imperative, and she clung to him, gasping, carried away by its sheer sensual force and the intense sensations it was already beginning to engender within her.

She began to move with him, learning the cadences of his passion and matching each stroke. Eagerly echoing the raw physical ebb and flow of their bodies' union. Striving to reach the coil of pleasure deep inside her and feel it gloriously unwind. Knowing it was there, but finding it strangely elusive.

She heard his breathing change and realised the momentum of his lovemaking had changed too, becoming faster, and threatening to leave her behind.

But, in the next instant, his hand slipped down between them to the joining of her thighs, finding her, touching her there— *there*—the caress of a fingertip enough to bring her, suddenly and fiercely, to sobbing, frenzied rapture.

And, at the very apex of her delight, she heard him call out harshly as he reached his own climax.

Afterwards, she lay wrapped in his arms, his head pillowed on her breasts, her body still glowing in the aftermath of consummation, and thought wonderingly—I'm a woman. Mark's woman.

Except that wasn't true, she reminded herself with a sudden pang, and she could not pretend otherwise. Because he'd simply done what she'd asked, no more, and now it was over.

And, almost as if he'd read her mind, he lifted himself carefully away from her and, without a word, left the bed, and then the room.

Tallie turned on her side, feeling desolation twist in the pit of her stomach. She put up a hand to touch her mouth, still tender from his kisses, then her throat tightened uncontrollably and she felt the first slow tears trickle down her face. And with a little sob she buried her face in the pillow.

The first inkling she had of his return was his hand on her shoulder, turning her towards him.

'Tallie?' He looked at her damp face and sighed as he rejoined her in bed, taking her swiftly in his arms. 'Oh, God, I did hurt you after all. I was afraid of that.' His voice was remorseful.

'No—no, you didn't.' Her head was against his chest, and his hand was stroking her tangled hair. 'I'm just being—stupid.'

'And probably in a state of shock too,' he said dryly. He was silent for a moment, then added quietly, 'Now, I think we should both try and get some sleep.'

Sleep? Tallie thought. How was that possible with her body, her mind and her emotions in such turmoil? And yet there was something ineffably soothing about his hand on her hair, and the steady beat of his heart under her cheek. And maybe she might rest—just a little—if she closed her eyes, and let herself drift on this warm, tideless sea of contentment…

When Tallie awoke there was daylight coming through the curtains. She lay for a moment, luxuriating in the feeling of well-being that was permeating her entire being, then turned, smiling, to look at him sleeping.

Only the bed beside her was empty, the pillows straightened and the covers tidy, as if she'd spent the entire night alone instead of in his arms.

And as if those unforgettable moments in paradise had never occurred. Were simply a waking dream. Except her body was telling her a very different story.

She slid her feet to the floor and fumbled her way into her robe.

Maybe he was just being considerate, she thought. Perhaps he'd decided his presence in her bed might prove an embarrassment in the cold light of day. That she might be regretting her recklessness of the previous night.

If so, she would soon set his mind at rest, she thought, and laughed softly to herself.

It was still early, she reasoned, so a visit to his room could bring its own rewards. And there was only one way to find out.

But he wasn't in his room. He was in the kitchen, fully dressed in dark suit, silk shirt and tie as he glanced though the newspaper.

'Good morning.' His voice was polite. No more. There was no hidden laughter there, or any shared knowledge in the cool green eyes that met hers. 'There's fresh coffee in the pot if you'd like some.'

She tried to think of something to say, but her mind was numb. She was icy-cold too, aware of an overwhelming need to wrap her robe ever more tightly round her, not simply for warmth on this sunlit morning, but to hide herself, just as if there was still one inch of her that he hadn't touched and kissed.

He picked up his briefcase and walked towards the door, and she felt herself shrink against the frame to avoid contact with him.

He added crisply, 'I'm off to Brussels. I shall probably be away for two to three days.'

She couldn't speak, couldn't find one rational word to say, so she nodded instead.

As he passed her, sending her—oh, God—a brief, impersonal smile, she could smell the faint aroma of his cologne and the warm, clean scent of his skin. The familiar essence of him that she'd breathed last night. Now—suddenly alien.

And, in spite of this, to her shame, Tallie found her body clenching in renewed desire.

As the front door closed behind him, she let herself slide down until she was sitting, huddled on the floor.

The floor where she knew she would have given herself to him again, if he'd shown any such inclination.

Only that wasn't the deal, she thought, staring blindly ahead of her. No part of the bargain she'd made with him.

What she had left—what she had to live with—was the resumption of their truce. Because that was what she'd promised him— that afterwards there'd be no expectations—no demands, so he was making absolutely sure that those terms were strictly adhered to.

Same roof—separate lives, she thought, just as before. His point made and thoroughly underlined a few moments ago. And nothing that had happened between them during that wild and beautiful night was ever going to make the slightest difference.

We were having sex, she thought, not making love, and I was a fool if I thought otherwise, even for a second.

And it was wonderful sex, because he wouldn't allow it to be anything less—not after those awful things I said to him. He was angry, and he had something to prove. Nothing else.

And I—I not only asked for it, I made it so easy for him, it was almost a bad joke.

Only I can't laugh about it. Because I'm angry too—with myself.

It would have been far better, she told herself bitterly, if he'd stayed away the first time he'd left her, reminding her of their agreement, and what she could expect. But he'd come back and held her while she'd slept, and somehow that was the cruellest thing of all.

She got to her feet and trailed to the bathroom, turning on the shower and standing under it, drenched and drowning, as she washed away any lingering traces of her abysmal folly and the subsequent humiliation that she so richly deserved.

Some of the water on her face was salt from the tears she couldn't control, but they were the last ones she would shed. She'd made a fool of herself, and worse than a fool, over Mark Benedict, but it was all over now.

And she had his absence of two—three days—to pull herself together. So that when he returned, he would find the positive avoidance of the last weeks re-established. She would be civil if they were forced to speak, and silent if they were not. Because pride alone demanded that she show him she could keep her word—and her distance.

As it had been, so it would be. Until the day she would thankfully go, and never have to see him again.

And if he insisted on intruding on her thoughts, she would deal with that too and also find some way of assuaging the quite ludicrous sense of hurt at this self-inflicted wound that was gnawing away at her.

I need to hate him, she thought slowly as she stepped out of the shower, wrapping her towel around her. And I think—in fact, I'm certain—I know exactly how I can achieve that.

And I may even find it a pleasure.

CHAPTER TEN

TALLIE stood watching the sheets of paper emerge from the printer, aware that she was shaking a little.

Because she'd finished it at last—the charged, ugly scene where the terrified and weeping Mariana was ruthlessly raped by Hugo Cantrell in revenge for losing the money he'd left with her. It was powerful stuff, probably the most dramatic piece of writing she'd achieved so far, pouring into it all her own pain, bitterness and disillusion about her night with Mark, and the total humiliation of its aftermath.

Although what they'd done together wasn't rape by any stretch of the imagination and she couldn't—wouldn't—pretend it was for an instant. On the contrary, she thought, wincing, she'd committed the ultimate act of lunacy in surrendering to him willingly, joyously, followed by the ultimate in self-deception—the brief and fatal hope that their encounter might mean something to him too.

Yet, at the same time, there'd been that telling moment when she'd been lying on the bed where Mark had thrown her, totally at his mercy, and she'd been scared. So she'd taken the feelings that had assailed her then and built on them, imagining the anger she'd sensed in him driving him on to some irrevocable and unforgivable conclusion.

Except it was Hugo, of course, who stripped the clothes from the frightened, struggling girl beneath him and took her with a cold brutality that spared her nothing, and left her shattered and alone.

Hugo, whom she'd made in Mark's image, originally as a joke. But which had suddenly become a far more serious issue.

At first, she'd been half-tempted to delete the whole thing, shocked at the anger and passion that screamed from her words. But then she reminded herself defiantly that she'd chosen quite deliberately to do this. To allow her story to give the pain inside her some sort of focus, and show Hugo Cantrell as the cruel and soulless creature he really was.

And she'd used him to some effect, although, as an exercise, she wasn't sure it had really made her feel any better. But while she wrote, she managed to provide herself with a mental barricade against unwelcome reality.

Because Mark Benedict was no loathsome fictional invention but a living, breathing man who would shortly be coming back into her life.

A man who had done exactly as she'd asked, and accepted her absurd assurances at their face value. And who'd promised nothing in return. A fact she could not escape.

But how could she possibly have foreseen how her night in his arms would make her feel—how her perspective would alter?

Yet she could not in reality blame him for that. It was entirely her own fault and, if she was angry, then she knew exactly where her rage should be directed.

The hurt and sense of loss were a different issue. And their intensity bewildered her. Even frightened her. And made her wonder how she would react when she saw Mark again.

He'd been away for over three days already and she told herself the longer his absence, the better, because it gave her more time to recover, and prepare herself to match his own indifference.

Brave words in daylight, but the nights were another story altogether.

Following his departure, she'd gone straight back to her room, stripped the bed completely and remade it, rigorously banishing every trace of him. At least that had been the intention. But, as she soon discovered, she could not remake her mind and her memory, or erase the new hunger in her awakened flesh.

She woke constantly in the darkness from restless, tormented dreams, reaching out to him, yearning for him, her lips eager for the taste of his skin, her hands recalling the dynamic of every bone and muscle in his lean, hard body. Only to find herself solitary and the bed beside her a wasteland.

But she should not—could not—allow herself to feel like that.

During the past twenty-four hours, she'd been particularly on tenterhooks, expecting at any moment to hear the front door open and his incisive step coming down the hall.

Especially, she acknowledged dryly, as, on practical terms, she was in his study, using his printer without permission.

But how could she ask someone who wasn't there? And, anyway, he'd be unlikely to object, she reminded herself. Because anything that would help her to finish the book and remove herself from his space would be fine with him.

Perhaps he was staying away so long because he half-expected her to break her word and confront him with the embarrassment of some girlish, emotional scene.

But that was a trap she would avoid at all costs.

Tallie turned away from the steady swish of the printer and looked around her. The room was no longer in the same pristine state as when she'd arrived. Even its atmosphere seemed to have changed, imbued with that restless energy that was so much a part of him.

The long table at one side of the room was littered with paperwork, as files and reports jostled for space with blueprints. While pinned to the wall above was a detailed map of the Buleza area, including the Ubilisi River.

It seemed he really intended to go back there, in spite of the increased risk from the new regime, Tallie thought, biting her lip. But he was his own man, with his own life, and if he wished to endanger himself it was no concern of hers. Nor could she allow it to become so.

When the printer was finally silent, she read through the final section, wincing a little, then added it to the folder with the rest of her completed pages. She'd written about two thirds of the book now, and for the first time she wasn't altogether certain of the direction it should take. Or not after the trauma of that last scene, anyway.

So the time had clearly come for the professional second opinion on the work in progress that Alice Morgan had offered.

'Yes, do let me see it,' had been her encouraging response to Tallie's tentative phone call earlier that day. 'You'll bring it round? Well, I shan't be here later, so leave it with my assistant and I'll read it as soon as I can.'

Which is going to be like waiting for sentence to be pronounced, Tallie thought as she fitted the folder into a padded envelope and added a covering note before setting off to the agency's office in Soho.

Her mission there was soon accomplished. The assistant, not much older than herself, said, 'Oh, yes, Miss Paget,' as if she was known and valued, instead of a floundering beginner, Tallie thought with amusement as she handed over the precious package. But it was gratifying just the same.

She didn't rush back to the flat afterwards, but went for a walk instead, lingering in front of shop windows and pausing to study the posters outside theatres, imagining a time when she might not have to count every penny.

Besides, now that she'd handed over the manuscript, she felt slightly bereft, she thought wryly. But until she heard from Mrs Morgan and was able to discuss with her the shape the book's ending should take, there was little she could do.

She stopped to read the menu outside an Italian restaurant but it only served to remind her that she was getting hungry, and it was time to return to Albion House and make herself some lunch.

She was just about to walk in the main entrance when a voice behind her said, 'Tallie, I thought—I hoped—it was you.'

She swung round, her eyes widening. 'Justin?' She forced a smile. 'What a surprise.'

'Not a horrible one, I hope.' His voice was rueful. 'I do realise

I may be the last person you want to see, but I think we need to talk. And I've brought lunch.' He held up a bag. 'A couple of chicken wraps. So may I come up to the flat?'

As she hesitated he added swiftly, 'Please, Tallie. Because you must be wondering about my weird behaviour the other night.'

'No,' she said hastily. 'Really. I—I quite understand.'

'You do? Did Mark explain?'

'No,' she said, wretchedly aware that her face was flaming. 'No, he didn't. It—wasn't necessary.' *But because of it I've done a crazy thing that I'll probably regret for the rest of my life.*

He sighed. 'I suppose you saw my reaction to Clive and guessed the rest.'

'Yes,' she said. 'Something like that.' *And I do not need to be having this conversation.*

'But not all of it,' he said. 'And that's what I need to tell you.' He paused. 'So will you listen?'

'Yes, I suppose so.' Her agreement was openly reluctant and she heard him sigh faintly as he followed her into the lift.

They sat in the kitchen to eat and, to her astonishment, she found she'd demolished every crumb of her wrap. Then she filled two mugs with fresh coffee from the percolator and sat down to listen, her face guarded.

At last, Justin said slowly, 'Firstly, I have to tell you that if I'd had the least idea Clive might be at Pierre Martin, we'd have gone somewhere else, but I didn't even know he was back in Britain.'

'Maybe you should also tell me why he seems to matter so much.'

'He was going to be my brother-in-law,' Justin said after a pause, his voice bitter. 'I was engaged to his sister Katrin, officially engaged with the diamond solitaire and a potential wedding date. We'd met six months before at a party, and she was the most beautiful thing I'd ever seen. She knocked me out, and when she agreed to marry me I told myself I didn't deserve to be so happy.

'I'd encountered Clive a few times, and not liked him much, but I told myself I was marrying Katrin not her relatives and, as they spent nearly all their time on a yacht in the Caribbean, they wouldn't be around to trouble us a great deal anyway.

'Her father I hadn't met at all up to then, but it wasn't a problem. I only had to convince him that I loved Katrin and was able to support her financially. Done deal. Or so I thought.'

He swallowed some coffee. 'I was fairly surprised to get a summons to Miami for our first meeting, but I'd already gathered from Katrin that Daddy was a high-powered fellow with his own way of doing things, so I didn't let it faze me.

'But I was disappointed that Katrin wasn't coming with me. She told me it was going to be man-talk, and that she'd be superfluous.

'So I flew to Miami and met Oliver Nelson at one of those vast luxury hotels. He seemed friendly enough, but I could tell he was sizing me up. Later, over dinner in his suite, he told me he was in the market for more than a son-in-law. That he wanted a business associate, and with my background in banking and accountancy I'd be ideal.'

He shook his head wearily. 'And then he told me what he wanted. Oh, he dressed it up a little, but it was money-laundering and we both knew it.'

He paused. 'So I told him—no, and I didn't dress it up at all. I also said I'd bring the wedding forward and make sure that Katrin saw as little as possible of him in the future.

'He—smiled. Who did I think, he asked, had suggested me in the first place?'

'No.' Shocked, Tallie put her hand on his. 'He couldn't have meant it.'

'Oh, but he did. And Katrin admitted it when I confronted her on my return. And what was so wrong anyway? she wanted to know. Wouldn't I like to be fabulously rich instead of just—well-paid?

'She said I was being offered an amazing opportunity, and she found my attitude—disappointing. And, by implication, I was disappointing too.

'When I was stupid enough to mention that our own plans seemed pretty wonderful to me, she looked at me without smiling and told me that, unless I did the deal with her father, we had no future. And, later that night, she moved out.'

Tallie swallowed. 'Justin—I'm so sorry. This is—unbelievable.'

'I thought so too, until I found out she'd taken the next plane to Miami, joining Daddy for a cruise on *Golden Aurora*. I realised then she'd meant every word.'

He looked at her. Smiled with an effort. 'That…was nearly a year ago. I've been working ever since at getting my life back together. I thought I was succeeding. And that meeting you—liking you, as well as fancying you rotten—was a major step towards full recovery.'

She said huskily, 'Justin, you don't have to say that…'

'Yes, I do.' His voice was urgent. 'Because it's the truth. God, Tallie, you must have known I had plans for that night. A new beginning with a bright lovely lady.'

She too forced a smile. 'Not just your See If I Care girl?'

'God, no,' he said. 'Far from it. In fact, I was so confident I was cured I even took you to Pierre Martin.'

'Of course,' she said slowly. 'You were with Katrin at its opening, weren't you, so it was a kind of test for yourself.'

He nodded. 'And everything was fine—wonderful—until Clive came up to the table. I thought I could deal with him, but it was his mention of a family party that did the damage, opened up the wound again. I had this overwhelming feeling that if I looked across the room, I'd see Katrin there.'

He looked ahead of him, his face blank. 'Of course, I knew it was bound to happen eventually. That, one day, we'd run into each other, but I truly believed that, by then, I'd be able to handle it.

'Only I suddenly realised I was fooling myself. That I didn't dare look across the room because I wasn't over Katrin at all. Because she was still there in my heart, and my bones. And I was scared, Tallie. Terrified I'd walk over to that table and agree to do any damned crooked thing her father wanted if I could just—*just*—have her back again.'

'And that's why you wanted to leave?' Tallie asked faintly. 'Not because of the other things he said?'

'By this point I wasn't really listening to the poisonous little bastard,' he admitted moodily. 'I just knew I needed to get out of there before I did something monumentally stupid and wrecked the rest of my life.'

She didn't look at him. 'I wish you'd told me at the time what was going on.' *Oh, God, if only—if only you had…*

'I should have done. I suppose I was too confused, and ashamed too. And that's why I came round today—to set things straight, if possible. And ask you to forgive me.'

'Of course I do.' She managed to speak lightly, crushing down the incipient hysteria that was bubbling inside her. 'Apart from anything else, I had a terrific meal, and there were no bones actually broken.' She held out her hand. 'So—friends?'

'I'd really like that.' He didn't release her fingers immediately. 'Tallie, I want you to know that if things were different…'

'Yes.' She freed herself gently. 'You're a lovely guy, Justin, and I know that in time you'll be ready to be happy again. With us, it was just too soon.'

I must have sensed that, she thought, as she came back after seeing him to the door. *And that was why I felt so uncertain about the prospect of sleeping with him. Because there couldn't have been any other reason.*

She went into the sitting room and dropped limply on to the sofa, sinking her teeth into her lower lip until she tasted blood. Wanting it to hurt.

How wrong, she asked herself numbly, *was it possible for someone to be?* She'd only been concerned with Clive's crude jibes about her age. But Justin, sinking back into the misery of the past, hadn't even heard them, and wouldn't have cared if he had.

But she'd jumped to conclusions and, in the process, had totally and fatally misunderstood the situation.

As Mark, of course, had suspected, even without hearing the full story from her. Because, of course, she'd never mentioned Clive. Which had been a mistake of the first magnitude.

Because, if I had, she thought. *If only I had—then he'd have* explained it all to me. Made me see that it was Justin's problem and had nothing to do with me. Would have told me that I must stop being paranoid about my age and lack of experience, sending me off comforted. I know he would. But I never gave him the chance.

Instead, I—I…

She gave a little choked cry, wrapping her arms tightly round her shaking body.

One of these days, she thought with anguish, Justin will tell his friend Mark all about that evening at Pierre Martin, and how Clive's intervention ruined everything. After all, why wouldn't he?

And Mark will think I simply invented everything I told him in order to get laid. A touch of illicit excitement to make up for my disappointing evening.

So now I don't just feel stupid. Because I've had sex with him under false pretences, and now, just thinking of the way he's going to look at me, I feel…dirty too.

And I just pray I'm long gone before that has a chance to happen.

She went slowly along to the bathroom, ran herself a hot tub and soaked in it for nearly an hour, wishing the soothing warmth could dispel the chill inside her.

Once dry, she wrapped herself in her dressing gown and lay down on top of the bed, her mind turning in endless circles without reaching any kind of resolution as regret, shame and every other negative emotion she could name went to war within her.

And this time she couldn't even hope for an uneasy truce, she thought with a pang.

She just had to hope that Mrs Morgan liked the book enough to show it to a publisher, and maybe get her some money up-front. Not a great deal, naturally, but enough to get her out of Albion House before Mark learned the truth.

Because if he thought badly of her already, his contempt would reach stratospheric levels after he'd talked to Justin.

And what could she say in her own defence?

But why do you need to defend yourself, argued a small voice in her head, when he's the Owner, the bastard, and the inspiration for Hugo Cantrell? What can his good opinion possibly matter?

I can't explain, she thought wearily, closing her eyes and turning on her side with a sigh. Not even to myself. I only know that it does matter—terribly. And I wish I knew why.

Tallie woke with a start, realising she must have dozed off, but assuring herself quickly that, if so, it could only have been for a few minutes. But the light in the room seemed to have changed quite fundamentally, and when she looked at her little clock she was startled to see that the supposed minutes were actually hours.

She sat up, listening intently. It was quiet everywhere, but even so she knew instinctively that she was no longer alone in the flat. That, at some point, Mark had returned.

And would, somehow, have to be faced.

Well, she told herself, swallowing, as she lifted herself off the bed, there's no time like the present.

But not in her robe, she amended quickly. That was what she'd been almost wearing the morning he'd left, and she didn't want to remind him of it.

She pulled on clean jeans and a sleeveless top, then, bracing herself, went to find him.

He was in the sitting room, stretched back on the sofa, a glass of whisky in his hand and a file of papers open but disregarded on the table in front of him, his brooding gaze fixed on space.

And then, becoming aware of her hesitating in the doorway, he rose coolly and formally to his feet.

'Hello.' Tallie came forward. 'I didn't hear you come in.'

'I've been back for some time. I'm glad I didn't disturb you.' His voice was expressionless, but she sensed a tautness about his tall figure, as if he'd also been dreading this first encounter.

Keep it friendly, she adjured herself. Keep it normal. Don't sound awkward or embarrassed. Above all, don't sound hopeful.

'I wasn't working,' she said. 'Actually, I was having a rest. I've done quite a lot to my book since you've been away.'

Now why had she told him that? she demanded silently and restively. Did she want him to recommend her for a Queen's Award for Industry?

He made no response, just stood watching her, the green eyes faintly narrowed.

She found his scrutiny disconcerting and hurried into speech again. 'So perhaps you'll soon have your flat to yourself once more.' Adding brightly, 'How was Brussels?'

'Much as usual,' he said. 'As far as I could judge between meetings.'

'So we've both had a busy time.' God, she thought, I sound like one of those talking dolls. Pull a string for today's cliché.

She waved a hand towards the file. 'And you're trying to work now, so I won't disturb you any longer.'

As he seated himself, his mouth seemed to twist in a faintly sardonic quirk. As if, it seemed to be saying, you could possibly disturb me on any level.

At the door, driven by some death wish, she paused again. 'Have you eaten?'

'I'm going out later.' His tone was crisp, warning her that she was straying on to forbidden ground. That food offers were still not part of the deal. Or friendly overtures, for that matter.

'Of course,' she said. *Of course, Sonia would be waiting. And, if not her, then someone else. Always someone else for the commitment-phobe.*

She was about to add, See you later, but refrained, reminding herself how unlikely it was that he'd be spending the night in his own bed.

Or in hers.

The thought came from nowhere, and with it a shaft of pain so swift and so deep that she almost cried out, needing all her self-command to take her out of the room, and out of his sight.

She made it back to her bedroom on unsteady legs, leaning against the closed door as she fought to calm her uneven heartbeat.

She said aloud in a voice that shook, 'Oh, God, what's happening to me? And how am I ever going to bear it?'

The summons from Alice Morgan came a week later. After what Tallie had mentally categorised as seven days from hell.

Since Mark's return, the tension between them had become almost tangible, exacerbated by his decision to work at home most days. In fact, the only respite had been provided by the visits of the cleaning lady, Mrs Medland, a cheerful, down-to-earth body, and the exact opposite of the dragon Kit had described.

At least Tallie had the odd friendly remark to look forward to when she was around, and it was like balm to the soul when Mark was barely acknowledging her presence.

It wouldn't be so bad, she thought, if she was still able to work on her book, but, for the time being, she was in limbo and, although she'd read and re-read her own copy of the manuscript every day, she still hadn't come up with any firm idea about how Mariana would deal with the terrifying trauma of her ordeal, or how she could take her story to a satisfactory conclusion after what had happened.

She tried to get out of the flat as much as possible, exploring London by long, rambling bus rides and going for lengthy walks. And in the evenings she spent much of her time in the breezy, crowded chaos of Lorna's flat in Hallmount Road, playing silly card games, listening to music, drinking cheap wine and talking about every subject under the sun, except her personal affairs.

But her carefree mood had usually dissipated by the time she got back to the flat, knowing that she would find it deserted and Mark gone for the night, leaving her to imagine in searing bitter detail who he was with and what they were doing.

Although it might not be Sonia's bed he was sharing, as Penny had ebulliently announced in another of her unexpected flying visits. 'Rumour has it that he cooled it a while ago, and she's peeved,' she'd said, her eyes dancing. 'Let's pray it's true and that he's found someone marginally human this time.'

Tallie could manage nothing more than a constrained smile in reply.

She was nervous about Mrs Morgan's verdict on her book, but at least it would give her mind a much-needed change of focus, she thought as she walked into the agency office.

Alice Morgan greeted her with a pleasant smile and an offer of coffee, which she gratefully accepted.

'Firstly,' the older woman began, 'let me say I'm excited about the way you've tackled this. There are a few places that could be tightened, but you seem to have a real grip on the story, and the action scenes you handle well. I was relaxing and thoroughly enjoying myself, then—whoosh, suddenly the whole thing careered off the rails into disaster.'

She shook her head. 'Tallie, my dear, I don't want to impose any modern political correctness on a story taking place two hundred years ago, but even so you *cannot* allow the hero to rape the heroine.'

Tallie stared at her. 'But he doesn't.'

Alice Morgan's brows lifted and she thumbed through the manuscript lying in front of her. 'Well, I don't know what else you call it, when a man ties a girl's hands together and forces himself on her repeatedly. When he hurts and degrades her in a way that, frankly, made my hair stand on end.'

'Yes, but it's Hugo Cantrell who rapes Mariana,' Tallie said with a touch of desperation. 'Because he isn't the hero—he's the villain.'

'The villain?' Mrs Morgan's voice was incredulous. She cast herself back in her chair. 'Oh, but he can't possibly be. He's absolutely gorgeous—to die for—and Mariana's clearly more than half in love with him already.

'No, he's clearly the hero, and has been ever since he rode up and caught her under the waterfall. You could have done rather more with that scene, by the way.'

She favoured Tallie with a long look. 'Promise me you're not still clinging to the idea of Mariana ending up with William the Wimp.'

'He's not like that,' Tallie said defensively. 'I—I realise I've neglected him rather, and he hasn't featured much in the story so far, but I can work on that. He has to be the hero. Mariana's loved him since childhood, and she's come all that way to find him.'

'She has indeed come a long way,' Mrs Morgan agreed. 'On a journey of self-discovery, no less. And, in the process, she realises where her heart truly belongs.'

She rolled her eyes to the ceiling. 'My dear girl, I can't believe you didn't realise this was happening. But I suppose the sub-conscious can play strange tricks.' She smiled. 'I won't ask what private fantasy inspired you to invent Hugo, but I'm very impressed.

'And, by the way you portrayed him, I thought you'd fallen pretty heavily in love with him yourself.'

'On the contrary,' Tallie said very clearly. 'I think he's absolutely vile.'

'Well, very few of your potential readers will agree with you there,' Mrs Morgan said briskly. 'And, whether you intended it or not, Hugo's taken centre stage in the book, and you have to leave him there.

'Besides,' she added practically, 'if he's genuinely so evil, why did he bother to save Mariana at the inn, when he could have got through the window himself and escaped? It makes no sense. Unless you want me to believe he was simply keeping her safe so he could rape her himself, which is nonsense.'

'But he's not just a rapist,' Tallie protested urgently. 'He's a traitor and a deserter, and he's going to murder someone, and be hanged for it.'

'I've no real objection to Hugo killing someone, if it's in the defence of the girl he loves.' Mrs Morgan tapped a finger thoughtfully against her teeth. 'Besides, the victim could be an Afrancesado—one of the Spanish who collaborated with Napoleon's troops, as could the men he cheated at the inn.

'As for him being away from the army, you could make him one of Wellington's exploring officers—military spies who infiltrated behind enemy lines for information on French plans. My brother's a military historian and he says it was highly dangerous work and they took the most appalling risks. The real stuff of heroes.'

She looked at Tallie and frowned. 'My dear, you look absolutely stricken. You've gone quite white. Are you ill?'

'No,' Tallie said hoarsely. 'Just—thinking.'

'And worried, I suppose, that you'll have to rewrite the whole thing?' Mrs Morgan's tone was understanding. 'A pretty daunting prospect, I agree, but I promise it's not necessary. Naturally, you'll need to change the emphasis in a few places, signalling Mariana's growing attraction to Hugo. No need to hold back on that any more.'

She paused thoughtfully. 'And, of course, the rape must go. But you can always replace it with a very different kind of love scene. Why not make it a seduction—with Mariana's full co-operation?'

She smiled at Tallie. 'I do realise it's not the story you set out to write originally, but it's going to work brilliantly.' She handed her a sheet of paper. 'I've made a note of some of my suggestions for you to work with. You don't have to go along with them all, but Hugo, I have to tell you, is not a variable. He has to be your hero.'

She rose. 'So I'll have the old script shredded and look forward to receiving the revised version. And if you have any problems, I'm on the other end of the phone. Good luck.'

Outside in the street, Tallie stood for a moment, dazedly gulping the thick, fume-laden air.

Mark and Hugo, she thought. Hugo and Mark. One fact, one fiction, who'd somehow become a single entity. Someone she'd wanted to dislike, had fought to hate, when every instinct had told her the opposite, as she'd travelled on her own unwitting journey of self-discovery. While she had battled to stifle the truth.

I thought you'd fallen pretty heavily in love with him yourself…

And so I did, she thought, as she began to walk slowly and aimlessly, struggling to come to terms with this hopeless, anguished self-revelation. So I always did—right from the start, when Tallie in the shower became Mariana under the waterfall, and found I was writing about feelings and desires that were totally alien to me, and that had to be denied.

But why didn't I realise they were happening to me?

Or have I've been lying to myself all along? And especially—that night…

Because I know now that I didn't simply want a lover, she told herself bleakly. I wanted *him*. Wanted him to belong to me and think only of me, even if it was just for a few short hours.

Because I believed that I could somehow make that enough. But I was wrong—so very wrong.

Pain twisted inside her as she remembered, too late, a favourite saying of her father's: 'Take what you want. Take it, then pay for it.'

So, I took, she thought, achingly. And now I shall end up paying in loneliness and unhappiness for the rest of my life.

CHAPTER ELEVEN

TALLIE delayed her return to the flat for as long as possible, knowing it would be harder than ever to face Mark now she'd been forced to confront the reality of her own emotions, and the pain this had engendered.

But at least she had the barrier of work to shelter behind once more, she thought as she made her way to the library and found a quiet corner where she read and re-read Alice Morgan's notes, her heart sinking. Re-creating Hugo as Mariana's beloved instead of her enemy wouldn't be that difficult, she thought wistfully. All she had to do was jettison the deliberate denial she'd been practising throughout the story so far, and write what was in her heart.

But providing the requisite happy ending for the lovers was a different situation altogether, because she'd be attempting to fulfil a dream that she knew was impossible. And she would need all the emotional strength she possessed, knowing that, with every word, she would be pressing down on the agony of an open wound.

Especially when the moment came for Hugo to look into his lady's eyes and say, 'I love you.'

But she would deal with that when she had to, she told herself with resolution. For now, she would look through the stock of books on the Peninsular war for references to exploring officers and their adventures. Concentrate on the practical stuff.

She stayed in the library until it closed, by which time her notebook was half-full of useful material, and Hugo's transformation didn't seem quite such a daunting prospect.

He would be faced with the terrible dilemma of trying to protect the girl he was growing to love without jeopardising the secret mission entrusted to him by Wellington.

While Mariana, of course, would be struggling to maintain her loyalty to the fading vision of William, and fighting her shameful attraction to a man she still believed to be totally unworthy.

Thinking it over, now that the first shock had worn off a little, Tallie had to admit that Mrs Morgan was quite right and the story would undoubtedly work much better like this. And, from now on, she told herself with determination, she would put out of her mind the reasons why Hugo had come to be invented and treat the whole thing as the pure fiction it always should have been.

As she waited to cross the road to Albion House, she saw Mark come out of the main entrance. He was walking with his head bent and, even from a distance, Tallie could see his expression was preoccupied, almost brooding.

She stood feasting her eyes on him, secure in the knowledge that she was unobserved. And realising, as she did so, that there was a kind of freedom in not having to pretend dislike or indifference any more. Except, of course, when he was standing in front of her, when the charade would have to be maintained. Even intensified.

She watched him hail a cab and drive away, trying hard not to speculate about his destination. But failing. Jealousy, she thought sadly, was one of the most negative emotions, but sometimes it was inevitable.

Because no one was fireproof and one day Mark would fall in love. Indeed, it could even be happening right now, and perhaps that was why he'd seemed so deep in thought—because he'd suddenly realised that 'commitment' was no longer a dirty word in his vocabulary. And maybe he too was struggling to come to terms with his discovery.

But, if this was so, it might be rather easier to bear when she was no longer around to be reminded on a daily basis that he had a life in which she couldn't hope for a part.

I need my independence, she told herself, swallowing. My own place to live, far away from here, and friends who have no connection with this period in my life. A whole new beginning. And, in order to achieve that, I have to stop confusing my emotional life with the necessity of earning my living, and offer Alice Morgan a book that she can sell.

So why don't I stop this futile hankering after a man I can't have, and get down to some work instead?

And squaring her shoulders, she crossed the road and went up to the flat.

By the time she fell into bed that night, Tallie could feel quietly satisfied with her evening's output, although making the required changes was not going to be an easy process and she still had a long and tortuous way to go. But she'd deleted all reference to the rape scene and felt oddly cleansed as a result.

After all, Mark had not asked her to fall in love with him, so it was wrong to denigrate him so appallingly in order to feel better about herself. Especially as it hadn't worked, anyway.

And she could use her own experience and emotions more usefully to illustrate Mariana's confusion of mind.

Although she was tired, sleep did not come easily. Instead, Tallie found she was dozing restlessly in fits and starts and around one a.m. she gave up the battle and lay wide awake, staring into the darkness.

Which would not do at all, considering the amount of work waiting for her. Maybe a milky drink would help, she thought, sighing.

She slid out of bed and put on her robe. As she opened her door and peeped into the passage, she realised that the kitchen light was on.

But maybe she'd forgotten to turn it off after she'd made herself the late toasted cheese snack, which might be to blame for her insomnia.

At the door, she halted, stunned by the sight of Mark, also in his robe, turning from the fridge with a carton of milk in his hand. And, before she could beat a hasty and silent retreat, he'd seen her too.

'Tallie.' He paused, frowning. 'Is something wrong?'

'No.' She moved forward hesitantly. 'I...I couldn't sleep, that's all.'

His mouth tightened. 'Nor could I.' He poured the milk into a pan waiting on the hob. 'I thought I'd have some chocolate. Do you want any?'

'Oh,' she said. Then, 'Yes—thank you.' She reached into the cupboard and took down the tin, but, when she held it out to him, he indicated silently that she should place it on the work surface and turned away to get the mugs.

My God, Tallie thought, her throat tightening, he doesn't want me anywhere near him. Not even to touch his hand in passing. And I cannot—must not—let him see that it matters—or if I've even noticed.

When all I want to do is run away and weep.

Instead, she went to the table and sat down, arranging the skirts of her robe decorously round her.

She said, making her voice casual, 'I didn't think you'd be here.'

'I'm catching an early plane.' His voice was clipped. 'I needed to pack.'

'Yes,' she said. 'Of course.' She paused. 'Is it going to be a long trip?'

'Possibly,' he returned. 'It's difficult to tell at this stage.' He poured the milk into the mugs and added the chocolate. 'But you know how to contact the lawyers if there's any problem.'

Suddenly her alarm bells were ringing as Tallie stared at him. She said quietly, 'It's the bridge, isn't it? In spite of everything, you're really going back to Buleza.'

'I never pretended otherwise.' He put her chocolate on the table in front of her and returned to lean against one of the fitted units. He added harshly, 'And you have no Veronica to impress this time, so you can drop the white-knuckled fears for my safety.'

She said huskily, 'I'm not even allowed to ask why you're deliberately putting yourself in danger?'

'It's not your concern,' Mark returned brusquely. 'But, for the record, there's nothing wrong with my sense of self-preservation. And the risk is minimal, or I wouldn't be going.'

He seemed to read the question in her eyes, and sighed impatiently. 'The new regime in Buleza is trying to make friends and influence people in the outside world, and they're not managing it particularly well. So, they'd have nothing to gain and a hell of a lot to lose by harming me, or any other foreign visitor. And, at the first sign of trouble, I shall be gone by the route we used last time.'

He put his mug down and left the room to return almost at once with the map she'd seen on his office wall, which he spread on the table in front of her.

'Buleza is frighteningly poor,' he said. 'And the people in the north are the worst off, because they're separated from what are laughingly thought of as the more affluent parts of the country by this—' he stabbed the map with a finger '—the treacherous and unpleasant Ubilisi River, which, as you can see, practically bisects the place. The bridge we were trying to build was no solution to their problems, but it was a first step.

'I need to see if anything can be salvaged from the original project, and if the new Democratic People's Republic wish to improve life for their northern compatriots by authorising the building of a replacement.'

He folded the map. 'I suspect I know the answer already, but I have to try.'

He paused, then added more gently, 'Now do you understand?'

'No.' Tallie got to her feet. 'But, as you've pointed out, it's hardly essential that I should.' She picked up the mug. 'I think I'll take this to my room and leave you in peace.'

'A curious choice of word,' he said. His smile grazed her. 'But probably a wise decision.' He looked her up and down, his mouth twisting cynically. 'Unless, of course, you were thinking of sending me off to my potential doom with a beautiful memory. And that's not very likely.'

'Not likely at all,' she agreed, keeping her voice bright. 'So—goodnight, and…good luck.' And went.

The chocolate was smooth and creamy, but it tasted as bitter as gall, and Tallie only managed a couple of mouthfuls. She could only think of Mark and the journey he was about to make.

He'd made comparative light of the risk involved, but she couldn't do so.

One of the broadsheets had profiled the new Bulezan president, and it had made grim reading. He'd had himself elected for life, and was dealing ruthlessly with anyone he saw as an enemy, apparently determined to rule by fear. And Mark had been rescued before by people he'd see as his opponents.

She lay on top of the bed, staring into space, her mind caught on a weary treadmill of love, loneliness and fear.

With Mark's departure went any immediate danger that she might betray herself to him, but that could be no comfort. Not any more. Because if the worst happened, she knew she would regret for the rest of her life that she hadn't been brave enough to confess to him her true feelings, chancing his mockery or his indifference. Enduring them if she had to.

And, as the sky began to turn light behind the curtains, she heard him walking quietly down the hall and knew what she had to do.

She was across the room in a flash, dragging open the door. At the sound he turned, his leather travel bag slung across one shoulder, his briefcase in his other hand. His surprise was evident.

He said tautly, 'I didn't mean to disturb you. I'm sorry.'

'You didn't,' she said. 'I was waiting.'

'Why? To say goodbye?' Mark's brows lifted. 'I thought we'd covered that already.'

'No, not—goodbye. That's too final. To ask you to take care, because if you…don't come back…if I never see you again, I won't be able to bear it.'

She saw the incredulity in his face and hurried on. 'And I'm sorry if that isn't what you wanted to hear, or if I've embarrassed you, and made you angry because I've broken our agreement.

'I…I just needed to tell you…to let you know how I feel, that's all, and now I've done so, it doesn't have to matter any more.'

She added huskily into the continuing silence, 'And I won't talk about it ever again, if that's what you want.'

'What I want?' The harsh query seemed torn from him. 'God almighty, Tallie, you pick your moments. All this wasted time—all those hellish lonely nights, and not one word—one sign until now—when I have to go and catch a bloody plane.'

He flung the travel bag and briefcase to the floor and came to her, pulling her roughly into his arms, his hands parting her robe to find the warm nakedness beneath it as he kissed her.

He was not gentle and she responded deliriously in turn, pressing herself against him, her arms locking round his neck as she gloried in the stark hunger that drove him, her body surging to his touch.

When he raised his head, they were both breathless.

He looked down at her, touching a rueful fingertip to the reddened and faintly swollen contours of her mouth.

He said, his voice unsteady, 'When I return, Natalie Paget, you and I are due for a very serious conversation.'

'Don't go.' She reached up to him, offering her eager lips, and he groaned softly as he kissed her again, his hand tangling in her hair, his mouth sliding down to the racing pulse at the base of her throat.

'I must, darling, and you know it.' He detached himself with open reluctance. Took her hand, touching her palm to his mouth. 'But sleep in my bed while I'm away—please,' he whispered against the soft flesh.

Then he stepped backwards, away from her, and walked across the hall to pick up his belongings.

At the door he turned. 'And I am coming back,' he told her, his sudden smile glinting in his eyes. 'So make sure you're here, and waiting for me.'

'Yes.' Her voice was a breath. 'I promise.'

After he'd gone, Tallie stood for a long time, staring at the closed door, feeling the blood sing in her veins, at the same time as the faint but potent ache of unsatisfied desire began to uncurl inside her.

But I can live with that, she thought, now that I have so much to hope for. When Mark comes back.

And, smiling in her turn, she went down the hall to his room. Discarding her robe, she slid under the covers of the big bed, then, turning her face into the pillow his cheek had touched, she fell deeply and dreamlessly asleep.

It wasn't always that simple, of course. There were nights when she couldn't shake off her anxieties entirely and lay for hours staring into the bleak darkness that his distance from her imposed.

By day, work came to her rescue. The astonished realisation and candid acknowledgement of her real feelings for him seemed to have opened some creative valve in her mind, allowing the words to pour out of her.

And it was surprisingly easy, she found, as the time following Mark's departure lengthened inevitably into weeks, to transpose her own emotions on to Mariana, burdening her with the frantic knowledge that Hugo, now her lover in every sense, was apart from her only because he was still deliberately endangering himself in Lord Wellington's service.

But, on the lighter side, there was also William, the book's erstwhile hero, to be dealt with. So, when Mariana eventually achieved her objective by reaching the British cantonments, Tallie enjoyed making him priggishly stuffy, and shocked to stiff-backed silence by what he regarded as the sheer and unforgivable impropriety of her quest. A totally unworthy object of her affection.

Unlike Hugo, who loved his wayward girl for what she was, rather than some dimly perceived pattern of feminine respectability.

And Tallie had worked out the book's ending too, forcing Hugo to face a firing squad at the demand of Wellington's Spanish allies for having murdered one of their number, a dashing young officer and sprig of the nobility whom he'd discovered was secretly in the pay of Bonaparte.

Which meant putting Mariana through the agony of witnessing Hugo facing his executioners, head high, his eyes unbound, before falling under the rattle of fire.

Except that none of the musket balls reached him, because the powder that dispatched them had been mixed with other less lethal substances at Wellington's order.

Something Mariana only learned when, listless and numbed by shock and grief, she entered the inn at Lisbon where she would stay before returning to England, and found Hugo waiting to go home with her, his work in the Peninsula over and done.

And Tallie was smiling through her tears as she sent them into each other's arms for the last time.

But she would have to wait for her own happy ending, it seemed, because Mark would not be returning any time soon.

The new President, it seemed, was graciously willing to meet him, but strictly in his own good time, as being measured for a wardrobe of new and splendid uniforms of his own design was taking precedence over everything else.

Or so she gathered down the crackling and echoing lines that suggested he was phoning from another planet. Because of this, their conversations were usually fairly abbreviated, and hardly romantic, but Tallie hadn't expected him to call at all, and so the regular sound of his voice, however brief and distorted, made her brim with shy delight. Especially as he tended to ring her late at night, as if deliberately waiting for a time when he knew she would be curled up in his bed.

But perhaps that was simply her imagination running riot, she thought wryly, and if so she needed to haul it back into line because it was needed for other purposes.

Alice Morgan had given the revised manuscript a brisk and unqualified commendation and announced she would be sending it out at once to selected publishers. Then, while Tallie had still been basking in the glow of that, she'd completely floored her by asking what her next book would be about.

'Because whoever buys it will want to know before offering you a contract,' she said. 'And almost certainly they'll be looking for another romantic adventure. So start thinking, my dear, and fast.'

Tallie had done precisely that, and had come up with a glimmer of an idea about a girl who takes to robbing stage coaches in order to clear her brother's name of some still amorphous wrongdoing, and finds herself facing a far more formidable adversary than the vagaries of British justice in the notorious highwayman Captain Moonlight.

She'd been to the library one afternoon to research crime and the underworld in the eighteenth century, and returned to the flat just as Mrs Medland was preparing to leave.

'You've a visitor, Miss Paget,' she said in an undertone, jerking her head significantly towards the sitting room. 'I told her no one was home, but she said she'd wait. Wouldn't take no for an answer either.'

Penny, was Tallie's immediate thought as she deposited her bag of books by the hall table. But, if it was, then Mrs Medland would surely have said. And Lorna, the other likely candidate, would still be at work.

Even so, she wasn't prepared to find Sonia Randall sprawled on the sofa, her hard eyes fixed on the doorway.

'So,' she said, 'if it isn't the budding authoress at last. Although that isn't quite accurate any more. Because I hear on the grapevine that you've bloomed—that your book is finished and starting to do the rounds. You must be very pleased with yourself.'

Tallie came forward warily. 'Good afternoon, Miss Randall,' she said, forcing politeness. 'I—I'm afraid Mark's still away.'

'Yes,' the other woman said. 'Playing the Good Samaritan in Africa again. But actually it was you I came to see.'

'Oh.' Tallie's heart sank like a stone. 'Then may I offer you some coffee—or tea, perhaps?'

'The perfect hostess.' Sonia's tone bit. 'And I'd have thought milk and water would be more appropriate—coming from you. However, I now realise one never can tell.'

Tallie lifted her chin. She said clearly, 'I don't know why you're here, Miss Randall, but I don't have to put up with your rudeness. Kindly see yourself out.'

As she turned, Sonia's voice halted her imperatively. 'I think you'd better sit down and listen, my girl. This is business, not social, and I have a lot more to say. I promise you're not going to like any of it.'

Tallie came back slowly and sat on the edge of the sofa opposite. She said coldly, 'If you're telling me Alder House isn't going to make me an offer, that's hardly a surprise. You made it clear you wouldn't be interested, and I informed Mrs Morgan accordingly.'

'I have no commercial interest in your scribblings, certainly, but I admit to being slightly curious—especially when we seem to share so much in other ways.'

The jibe was hardly unexpected, but Tallie winced inwardly all the same. She made her tone dismissive. 'I hardly think so.'

'Oh, don't be coy. I had a look round while the cleaning woman was busy in the kitchen, and I noticed that the spare room is now just an office. I also saw there were things of yours in Mark's room.'

Tallie moved restively. Much as she disliked the other woman, she realised that she must be hurting too. 'I—I'm sorry.'

Sonia shrugged. 'Why? It's no surprise. It was perfectly obvious at the dinner party from hell that he was planning to bed you. Unless, of course, his mate Justin managed to get there first, but Mark enjoys a challenge, and my money was on him.'

Tallie stared at her. 'You mean—you don't care?'

'What is there to care about? Mark likes variety in his bedmates—I've always known that—and you must have been a real novelty.' She added softly, 'But although I also know he likes to play rough at times, the fact that you appear to share his taste really has surprised me.' She laughed. 'I'd have said you were much too prim for those games.'

Tallie suddenly felt cold. 'I don't know what you're talking about.'

'Then let me refresh your memory.' Sonia reached into the large suede bag at her feet and extracted a bulky file which she placed on the table between them. 'After all, it's here in black and white. Or should I say in vivid, glorious detail. Tell me something.' She lowered her voice intimately. 'Was it Mark's idea to tie you up, or yours?'

Tallie stared at the file in horrified recognition. It was her original manuscript, she thought, nausea rising within her, complete with that dreadful rape scene—the one Alice Morgan had promised to shred. Yet—somehow—here it was.

She said hoarsely, 'Where did you get that?'

'From your agent's office. I had it collected by messenger. Apparently it was the very last copy, and I read it with total fascination, especially the final chapter. Does Mark actually know that his more unusual sexual proclivities are going to appear in print, or are you planning to surprise him?'

'But it's fiction,' Tallie said wildly. 'I—I invented it. All of it. Everything.'

'Not quite everything, my dear,' Sonia drawled. 'Your description of the Cantrell character is Mark to the life, including those very distinctive scars. Certainly no fiction there, so why shouldn't the rest be true?'

Tallie tried to steady her voice. 'Because you of all people should know that it isn't. That Mark never…' She drew a breath. 'That he wouldn't—*couldn't*…'

Sonia leaned back, smiling. 'I only know he didn't with me. But then he didn't see me as a victim. Maybe that makes a difference.'

Tallie said quietly, 'You're vile. Utterly beneath contempt.'

'And you're Snow White, I suppose.' The older woman's tone grated. 'Except she never found herself in court facing an action for libel.'

Tallie gasped. 'What are you talking about?'

'About Mark's reaction when this garbage—' she pointed at the folder '—is made public.'

'But it never will be,' Tallie said desperately. 'I rewrote the whole thing and it's completely different. Hugo Cantrell has become the hero. That…episode has gone.'

'Gone?' Sonia echoed. 'When I've read it, and other people can too? I hardly think so.'

'But no one else is going to read it,' Tallie argued. 'This is the only copy.'

Sonia shook her head slowly. 'It was, perhaps. But not any longer, because I can think of a couple of seriously downmarket tabloids who'd love to get some dirt at last on the great Mark Benedict.'

'On Mark?' Tallie queried in bewilderment. 'But why should they care about him?'

Sonia looked at her for a long moment, then began to laugh. 'Why, Natalie Paget, I do believe Mark's been holding out on you. I admit this run-down pad isn't the kind of environment you expect for someone who's a millionaire several times over, but it belonged to his mother and he feels sentimental about it. God knows why.'

She shrugged. 'He doesn't make a fuss about his money, of course. Likes to see himself as a co-worker in all those companies of his, and not just the boss. And, in his way, he's quite a philanthropist, although he invariably denies it because he loathes publicity.

'He refused point-blank to do any "millionaire hero" interviews after he got his men out of Buleza, and wasn't terribly polite about it, according to a friend of mine who's been looking to get her own back.

'So imagine how he'll feel when he finds himself the centre of a sordid sex scandal—featuring as the incredibly rich man who raped his cook, the innocent virgin he took off the streets. And how she got her revenge by detailing her ordeal in a cheap bodice-ripper.'

'But there isn't a word of truth in it,' Tallie said stonily. 'And I shall say so.'

Sonia laughed again. 'Oh, you've said too much already, my child.' She leaned forward, tapping the manuscript with a crimson nail. 'And it's all here. And even if Mark can get the all-powerful lawyers he employs to stop the papers printing the story, the word will still get around—my friend will see to that—and the damage will be done.

'Because some people will actually believe it, some will always wonder, and some will laugh. And I wonder which reaction Mark will hate the most?' Her smile lapped at the cream. 'But, more importantly, what's he going to say to you, little Miss Paget, and what will he do? You've invaded his precious privacy, dented his reputation and made him look ridiculous, which is something he'll never forgive. And if you think otherwise, you don't know him. And it won't matter a damn what you're prepared to do with him in bed.

'So, he may well decide to teach you a lesson through the courts. I hope your family has money, because the damages could be substantial.

'And as Mark won't want to feature as either hero or villain in your adolescent ramblings, he'll probably get an injunction to stop you publishing the other version too.

'Not that you'll find a market anyway,' she added. 'Publishers cringe at the word "libel" and your precious agent won't be too pleased to know that the ludicrous Hugo is based on a real life model.'

She gave a contented sigh. 'So, my dear Natalie, I'd say your little romance is dead in the water, and your writing career is toast. What do you think?'

CHAPTER TWELVE

'You want to withdraw the manuscript?' Alice Morgan repeated, her tone and expression aghast. 'But my dear child, why?'

Tallie looked down at her hands, twisted together in the lap of her cream skirt. She'd been reluctant to wear the outfit Mark had bought her, but she'd forced herself to put it on because it was important to be dressed properly for this crucial interview. To look as if she was actually in charge of her own life, and not the pathetic loser she knew herself to be.

'It's just the decision I've reached,' she said in a low voice. 'I've realised I don't want to make writing my career after all, so there won't be another book, and I can hardly offer the first one under false pretences.'

'But you were so eager,' Mrs Morgan said unhappily. 'And you have real talent too. It's turned out to be a splendidly rip-roaring read.' She paused. 'Are you sure you're not just suffering a sense of anticlimax now that the book's finished? Or worrying, perhaps, in case no one wants it? Because you're quite wrong about that, I assure you. I have two editors interested already, and a third is telephoning me this afternoon. It may even go to auction.'

Tallie suppressed a shudder. 'Then stop it—please. I...I can't let that happen.'

Because she had to live with the possibility that Mark might do exactly as Sonia had suggested, and take some kind of legal action, with the kind of far-reaching consequences that night-mares were made of.

Mrs Morgan sighed. 'I wish you'd tell me what the problem is. Perhaps we could solve it together.'

And I wish I could explain, Tallie thought desolately, but I can't. This is the deal I've been forced to make with Sonia Randall and, for Mark's sake, I have to stick to it. I must do exactly as she says, because anything else—seeing his name dragged through the gutter press—knowing that people are talking—laughing about him—is unthinkable.

I can't bear to think what I've done to him already, or that she knows about it. I could have ruined everything for him, made him an object of ridicule. So, instead, I have to kill off my book com-pletely and get out of his life. Never see him again.

That was what Sonia eventually demanded, and I—I had to agree. I didn't have any other choice.

Not that he'll want anything more to do with me once Sonia shows him that original manuscript with that cruel, horrible scene in it. And she intends to. I couldn't talk her out of it, even though I begged. And he'll hate me for it—*hate me*…

But will he like her any better? She'd certainly seemed to think so, Tallie thought, remembering the gloating triumph in the older woman's face.

'Mark can be completely ruthless when crossed,' she'd said as she'd prepared to leave. 'And don't think spending a couple of nights in his bed will make him any more merciful when he dis-covers the truth. He's always been well out of your league, my dear, so find some children of your own age to mix with in future, and be thankful you're getting off so lightly.'

But, thought Tallie, it didn't feel like a fortunate escape. Quite the opposite, in fact.

Through the sudden tightness in her throat, she said, 'I've changed my mind, that's all. Decided to get a real job instead of wasting time indulging my adolescent fantasies.'

She got a shrewd look from the other side of the desk. 'Now

that sounds as if you're quoting someone else's opinion. Is that what it is?'

Tallie forced a smile. 'Or maybe I've discovered what hard work writing is, and realised that it's not for me.'

Mrs Morgan sighed. 'I certainly don't believe that—not when you turned round the book so quickly after our chat. And came up with another idea at once. But clearly you've taken a hell of a knock for some reason.'

She paused. 'However, I urge you not to do anything rash. To set your mind at rest, I'll recall the scripts that I've sent out and put the whole thing on hold for a while. Will that do?'

'Because you think I'll change my mind?' Tallie shook her head. 'I won't. In fact, I'm leaving London altogether. Today.'

And going home to hide. If I tell them I couldn't hack it, they'll accept that and, because they love me, they won't press me about it.

'If I never see you again, I won't be able to bear it.' That's what I told him, and now I'm having to face the stark reality that I've lost him. Face it—and somehow deal with it.

And one day this pain—as if someone has put a hand in my chest and wrenched out my living heart—will begin to get easier.

At least I have to believe that, or I couldn't go on.

Mrs Morgan rose. 'In that case, all I can do is wish you luck.' She clasped Tallie's hand for a moment. 'But I still wish you'd felt able to confide in me, my dear.'

Tallie muttered something incoherent and turned to the door. She couldn't confide in anyone, she thought wretchedly. Not now. Not ever. And knowing that there'd been a real possibility of her book being published only added to her burden of unhappiness. And her sense of failure.

She hadn't even asked why the original version hadn't been shredded as arranged, because she knew. Mrs Morgan's usual assistant was off sick and there was a harassed temp manning the outer office, so it was pointless trying to apportion blame.

Her case, containing everything she possessed, was also in the outer office with her laptop. Before leaving the flat, she'd left money for her share of the bills as she'd always intended. Plus a note that said simply, 'I'm sorry.' Which she hadn't intended, or ever thought would be necessary.

After telephoning her mother to say she was returning, she'd called Hillmount Road and left a message on Lorna's answering machine saying merely that she was going away for a while, and she'd be in touch. Apart from that, she spoke to no one.

Penny might wonder what had happened to her for a time, she thought, but London was a shifting community. People came and went, and were eventually forgotten.

And maybe it was those who left who took their memories with them.

Memories that were already haunting her as she sat on the train, staring at the fleeing countryside with eyes that saw nothing.

I'm sorry...

What exactly was she apologising for when she'd scrawled those two desperate words? she wondered drearily. For breaking her promise to be there when he returned, her body eager— yearning for his hands—his mouth? For re-inventing him as Hugo in a fit of childish resentment? Or for that fatal desire to punish him for hurting her in the icy aftermath of that one glorious night they'd spent together?

The list seemed endless. Not that Mark would care. Not once he'd heard what Sonia had to tell him. She could imagine his face hardening implacably as he crushed the note in his fingers. No man liked to be made a fool of, and powerful wealthy men would hate it most of all.

And she would be easily replaceable.

There would always be willing women to share his bed. Women who would not expect—or hope—for too much from him in return, as she'd been in danger of doing.

And perhaps it was best that it should end now, before she could damage herself even further. Because, as Sonia had pointed out, she was not in his league.

Besides, nothing he'd said in those last passionate moments

before his departure, or in those brief exchanges from Buleza's collapsing phone system indicated anything more than his desire to make love to her again.

She remembered the last time they'd spoken, only two evenings ago, when he'd paused before saying goodbye to ask what she was wearing, and she, stretching languidly against the cool sheets, had told him, 'Nothing.'

And heard the rueful amusement in his response, 'Oh, God, another sleepless night.'

And she'd smiled too, cradling the phone against her cheek, as her own need ran like wildfire through her veins and tingled along her nerve-endings.

But she doubted whether the thought of her naked in his bed would keep him awake for too long. Any more than she could honestly believe in the 'wasted time' or 'hellish lonely nights' that he'd spoken of. He must have spent them somewhere, she thought unhappily, and with someone. It might even have been Sonia…

And she was totally naïve to think otherwise.

If only I'd stayed in my room that morning, she whispered silently. If I'd remained in control of my emotions and let my head rule my heart, instead of giving way to my longing for him.

But it was too late for this, or any of the vast multitude of regrets that were eating away at her like acid into metal.

And at least she would spend tonight in her own bed, she thought, and not lying on the mattress in the spare room, wrapped in a duvet. And there would be no need to clamp her hands to her ears in an effort to shut out the sound of the phone ringing and ringing down the hall in Mark's empty bedroom.

Had he wondered why she didn't reply, and why the answering machine was switched off? Or had he simply shrugged and turned away, his mind already switching to other, more immediate problems?

And would it ever occur to him, when he found her gone, that she hadn't taken his call or let him leave any message because it was impossible for her to endure the knowledge that she'd be listening to the sound of his voice for the last time?

No, she thought. That aching awareness would be hers alone.

And, like so much else, would have to be kept hidden behind the smiling face she needed to show when her journey ended, and she was home again.

'You've lost weight, darling,' Mrs Paget chided, and Tallie pulled a face.

'You always say that.'

'Because it's always true,' said her mother, adding cheerfully, 'but some decent food will soon have you back in top condition.'

'Like a prize heifer on her way to market,' Tallie teased, and hoped that the forced note in her voice wouldn't be noticed.

'You also need new clothes,' Mrs Paget went on, frowning a little. 'I'll get Dad to give you your birthday cheque early, and we'll go shopping.' She tutted over the meagre display taken from Tallie's case and laid out on her bed. 'There's nothing fit to keep. Not even the charity shop would give you thanks for it—apart from the skirt and top you're wearing, of course, which are lovely—and pricey too, like those gorgeous sandals. How on earth did you manage them?'

'They were on special offer,' Tallie said, and turned away to hide the tell-tale warmth invading her face. 'But I'll keep my working skirts and blouses. I'll need them when I find a job.'

'Well, there's no hurry for that,' Mrs Paget decreed. 'As soon as I saw you get off the train, I noticed your eyes were really peaky.' She shook her head. 'No, you're in need of a good rest, my love, and that's what you're going to have. I never thought London was healthy,' she added dismissively, and departed to make the steak and kidney pie she'd promised for supper.

Oh, God. Tallie thought, sinking wearily down on to the cushioned window-seat. Her attempt at a jaunty façade seemed to be cracking already. But then mothers could make the average eagle seem positively myopic.

But getting herself into full-time employment, and soon, was essential.

I have to keep busy, she thought desperately. Have to do everything possible to stop myself thinking—brooding. Grieving.

And there'd be other problems too. On the drive back from the station, her mother had mentioned over-casually that she'd seen David Ackland's mother in the supermarket earlier.

So I can expect a call from him, no doubt, she decided resignedly. And what possible excuse can I make? Sorry, David, but I've given myself body, heart and soul to a man whose life I nearly destroyed, and whom I'll never see again, is hardly a viable option, with Mum probably not far away, checking discreetly on her attempt at matchmaking.

But I doubt if he'd be prepared to be my See If I Care man either, even if I felt brave enough to consider it.

Sighing, she leaned her forehead against the cool window pane.

'Mark,' she whispered achingly. 'Oh, Mark, why did I have to love you, when it hurts so much to let you go?'

And knew she would never find an answer.

The days dragged past. The weather turned to rain and there was a morning chill in the air that spoke of autumn. In spite of the weather, or maybe because it matched her mood so closely, Tallie spent as much time as possible out of doors, taking the grateful dogs for longer and longer walks.

She was aware that her mother had begun to watch her with puckered brows, and feared that soon there'd be some form of gentle, but searching inquisition about the past months in London.

Naturally the subject of her abortive writing career had been raised—over supper on her first evening—but her parents had seemed to accept her explanation that things simply hadn't worked out.

'Such a pity when that lady agent seemed to think so highly of you,' had been her father's quiet comment. And after that the matter, thankfully, was allowed to drop.

In between helping to make blackberry jelly, pick apples and gather hazelnuts, Tallie tried to infuse some zip into the CV accompanying the job applications she doggedly sent off, but was not surprised when she was not interviewed for any of them. Maybe her lack of enthusiasm was as obvious as a finger mark on wet paint, she surmised wryly.

And maybe she should seriously consider her father's suggestion that she consider her time in London as a gap year and return to some form of higher education.

It was a supremely sensible idea, if only she'd been able to contemplate what shape her future might take, but, at the moment, that was beyond her. She couldn't think further than the next day.

In the meantime, she'd managed to get evening work, waitressing in the local pub which had a popular restaurant, and this had the added advantage of keeping David Ackland's gently persistent phone calls at bay, as well as earning her some money.

She'd been at home for nearly a fortnight when a large cream envelope arrived in the morning post, and Mrs Paget's eyebrows shot up as she examined the flamboyantly engraved card it contained.

'Good God,' she said blankly. 'Your cousin Josie's getting engaged—and to Gareth Hampton, of all people. The one who was always so full of himself when his family lived here. I'd no idea they knew each other. In fact, I was rather afraid you were developing a thing about him yourself at one point.'

'Well, not any more, and everyone's allowed at least one deliberate mistake.' Tallie made herself speak lightly. 'I presume there's going to be a big party?'

'Yes.' Her mother gave the card a last dubious look and put it down. 'And you and Guy are invited to bring your partners.' She brightened. 'Why don't you ask David to go with you? He's such a nice boy, and worth ten of Glamorous Gareth.'

'Or I could simply not go at all,' Tallie suggested, as she got up from the kitchen table. 'Anyway, we'll talk about it later,' she added, as her mother's lips parted in protest. 'It seems to have stopped raining for five minutes so I'll take the dogs out.'

It was an eventful hour, involving the pursuit of real or imagi-

nary rabbits through a muddy copse, an encounter with a neigh-
bour's cat, who simply climbed a tree and sneered at them, and a
totally unscheduled dip in the river, before an exasperated Tallie
called them sternly to heel and started for home. Upon which, the
heavens opened, drenching her to the skin in minutes.

As she opened the back door, the dogs shot past her, skittering
through the kitchen, with its seductive scent of home-baking, and
down the passage to the front of the house, where she could hear
them barking joyfully.

Her mother turned from the stove, looking unusually flurried.
'Tallie, there's someone to see you. He arrived a few minutes ago,
so I put him in the sitting room, but it sounds as if Mickey and Finn
have found him, so maybe you'd better rescue him while I make
some coffee. And ask him if he'd like a hot scone.'

Tallie pushed back her tangle of sodden hair with a resigned
hand. David Ackland, no doubt, she thought, missing out on his
Saturday morning at the squash club to become the joint victim of
a maternal conspiracy. The phone line between here and Myrtle
Cottage must have been glowing red hot in the past hour.

Be pleasant but firm, she adjured herself as she walked down
the passage. But make it clear that neither of you will be going to
Josie's bash.

And then she walked into the sitting room and saw the tall
figure standing by the rain-soaked window, the object of the
dogs' vociferous welcome. And her mouth dried and the room
swam dizzily around her as she realised exactly who was
waiting for her.

'Mark.' The name emerged as a croak. 'You.'

'Full marks for observation.'

It was not a promising start. She said quickly, 'I'm glad you're
safe. Are—are you going to build your bridge?'

'Not under the present regime. The new president is planning
a palace instead, a cross between a brothel and the Taj Mahal.'

'You must be disappointed.' She took a deep breath.
'What…what are you doing here?'

'Looking for you.' His dark face was unsmiling. 'I did say I'd want a serious conversation with you when I came back. If you remember.'

'Yes.' Tallie swallowed. 'But the circumstances have changed since then.'

'I'm well aware of that.' The dogs were still leaping rapturously around him, but he snapped his fingers and they subsided, plumy tails beating the rug with rhythmic pleasure as they gazed up at him.

She heard herself say inanely, 'The dogs have been in the river.'

'You look as if you went with them,' he commented expressionlessly. 'Maybe you should dry your hair and change your clothes before we talk.'

She shook her head. 'If I leave this room, I may not have the courage to come back.' She lifted her chin. 'I'd much rather you said what you came to say—so I know the worst.'

'The worst,' Mark repeated slowly. 'Now, there's an interesting choice of words.'

She stared at the floor. 'I realise how angry you must be, and I accept the blame for that. Totally. And I'm terribly ashamed.'

Her mouth trembled. 'I suppose, for all my denials, I am still a child after all. A stupid, destructive child who takes something precious and smashes it, without realising it's gone for ever. And if I could go back in time and not write those horrible things, I would.

'But I can't, and I suppose you could still sue me for libel, because Sonia read what I wrote, and she's threatening to show other people. But—oh, God, Mark—my parents know nothing about all this. I...couldn't tell them, and if I end up in court, it will nearly kill them. And if there are damages, I won't be able to afford them.'

'Well, I wouldn't worry too much about that,' Mark said calmly. 'I believe a husband is still considered responsible for his wife's debts, and paying damages to myself seems a pretty futile exercise.'

The room swam even faster. Tallie made it to the sofa and sank down on the cushions. She stared at him.

'What—what are you talking about?'

'Marriage,' he said. 'You must have heard of it. Exchange of rings—till death us do part—a home—babies? Strike any chords?'

'But you don't want to marry me,' she said, her voice shaking. 'You can't.'

His brows lifted. 'Why not?'

'Because you could have anyone. Your—Miss Randall told me that you're a multimillionaire.'

'Yes,' he said. 'Although I wasn't actually planning to buy you. And I know a lot of people far richer than I am,' he added. 'I'll introduce you to a few and you can compare notes.'

She beat her hands together in frustration. 'Oh, be serious.'

'Tallie,' he said very patiently, 'this is the incredibly serious conversation I mentioned before I went to Buleza. Asking you to marry me. Didn't you realise that?'

'But you don't commit.' Her voice was almost a wail. 'Penny said so.'

'Pick a church, name a day, and watch me,' Mark retorted. 'You can ask Penny to be a bridesmaid. Now, my darling, will you stop talking to other people and listen to me? Please?'

He paused. 'I admit,' he said slowly, 'that marriage wasn't my priority when I first met you. Not until we made love, and I woke up at dawn with you in my arms and lay there, watching you sleep. You were smiling a little and I knew, as certainly as I drew breath, that was how I wanted to wake every morning for the rest of my life with you—my wife—beside me.

'And, for a few brief moments, I was completely happy, until I remembered that you didn't feel the same. That, to you, I was nothing but the tame stud you'd asked to ease you out of your inconvenient maidenhood. Also that you'd made it very clear this would be the only night we'd ever spend together.

'Which was when I realised I'd fallen into the appalling trap of loving a girl who didn't want me in return.'

'But when I came to find you, you were so cold,' she whispered. 'You hardly looked at me—or spoke.'

'I was terrified. I was praying that you'd smile again and come across to me. Or at least put out a hand.' His tone was matter-of-fact. 'But you just stayed in the doorway, without a word, looking at me as if I was an unexploded bomb.' His mouth twisted. 'So, no change there. And, as I walked past, you practically cowered. I was bloody devastated. I must have sleepwalked through those days in Brussels because I hardly remembered a thing about them when I came back.

'I could only think— She doesn't love me. She'll never love me…'

He paused again. 'And then there was Justin, of course.'

'Justin?' Tallie echoed. 'But nothing happened between us. You knew that.'

'But I saw him leaving,' he said, 'the day I got back. I was paying off my taxi when he came out, and I thought he'd—been with you. That he'd persuaded you to forgive him and you'd decided he was the man you wanted after all. That I'd been the rehearsal, but he was the main performance.

'I also realised I wanted to beat the living daylights out of him. So I got back into the cab and told the guy to drive—it didn't matter where.

'When I came back, the flat was full of the scent of that bath oil you use. I opened your door and you were asleep on the bed wearing nothing but that bloody cotton dressing gown.'

He drew a harsh breath. 'Christ, my imagination went into overdrive. All I could think of was—the two of you—together, sharing the pleasure we'd known. That you'd been mine, and I'd lost you. Let you go, when I should have fought for you.'

He shook his head. 'I didn't know I could feel quite so violent towards one of my best mates. Jealousy's a terrible thing.'

'You—jealous?' There was incredulity in her voice, and his smile was wry.

'It came as quite a shock to me, too. But then so did being in love.' He paused again. 'By the way, who the hell is "poor David"?'

'Someone in the village. Why?'

He shrugged. 'Because when your mother answered the door

and I asked for you, she gave me a very long look, said "Poor David", then showed me in here. She also offered me some coffee,' he added thoughtfully. 'But it hasn't appeared.'

She said guiltily, 'I was supposed to ask if you want a hot scone.'

He smiled at her. 'I'd much prefer twenty-four hours of total seclusion, and you without your clothes. But, for now, I'll settle for food and drink. Thank you.'

'I'll tell her.' She stood up and moved to the door.

'And don't run away again,' he called after her. 'You've just given me the worst week of my life.'

Mrs Paget was sitting at the kitchen table absorbed in a book that she slid under a tea towel when she saw her daughter. But not before Tallie had seen the title, *Cooking for Special Occasions.*

If she's reading the section on wedding cakes, she thought grimly, I shall stab her with her own icing nozzle.

She looked around. 'Didn't you make any coffee for Mr Benedict after all?'

'It can be ready in minutes.' Her mother rose. 'I thought you wouldn't want to be interrupted.'

'I've been flat-sitting for him while he's been in Africa,' Tallie said evenly. 'He—had some questions for me.'

'Then he's come a long way to ask them,' Mrs Paget said affably. 'Also he has the same lost, desperate look that you've been carrying around since your return.' She paused. 'When I bring the tray, I'll knock.'

Tallie went back to the sitting room, closed the door, leaned against it and said, 'Mark, I can't marry you.'

'Has your mother forbidden the banns?'

'Far from it,' Tallie said bitterly. ''It's—just impossible, that's all. It can't happen.'

'Because you don't love me?'

She said in a low voice, 'You know that isn't true. I've been feeling only half alive since I left. But how can you want me—after what I did?'

'You haven't done anything.'

She gasped. 'You mean Sonia Randall didn't show you the first draft of the book. The one where I—I…'

'Described me as the epitome of evil?' Mark supplied. 'Yes, I read it, and was enjoying your portrayal of me as arch-villain until that last scene which, I admit, shook me.

'I realised you must have written it after we'd made love, and I asked myself if there was anything that had happened between us that could have been construed as rape. If I'd—disgusted you in some way.'

'Mark…' Her voice thickened.

'And then,' he went on, 'I recalled a moment when I could easily have lost all control—and I'd let you know it. I also remembered what I'd said to you, and felt sick to my stomach.

'It occurred to me, too, that when I was carefully distancing myself from you for my own self-protection, I might have hurt you very badly. That making me out to be a total bastard could be a defence mechanism on your part.

'Most of all, I realised how scared you must have been to break your promise to wait for me, and run away.'

Tallie wrapped her arms round her body. She said in a low voice, 'She—Miss Randall—said dreadful things. I was afraid she'd get her reporter friends to write stories to make it seem as if you'd actually raped me—and the book was my revenge. That people would think there was no smoke without fire, and you'd hate me for damaging your good name.'

He said very gently, 'Darling, I could never hate you, whatever you did. And the only opinion about me I value is yours.' He smiled at her. 'And I was glad to know that you redeemed me in the second draft.'

Her lips parted in shock. 'You read that too?'

'I certainly did.' His smile widened reminiscently. 'I particularly liked the scene at the waterfall. It reminded me that we've yet to take a shower together, something I feel we should put right very soon.'

There was a note in his voice that sent her colour soaring. She said hurriedly, 'But how did you get hold of the book? There wasn't a copy at the flat.'

'Alice Morgan gave it to me. Incidentally, her reaction when I walked into her office was even more interesting than your mother's. She sat back in her chair and laughed until she cried.'

'You went to see Mrs Morgan?' She froze.

'She was my last hope,' he said. 'No one else knew where you'd gone. I even steeled myself to go to Justin and check if you were with him. That note you left was pretty ambiguous. You might have been saying, Sorry—I've decided I picked the wrong man. I told myself that if you'd gone to him, I'd learn to deal with it somehow, because at least you'd be safe.

'However, after he'd put me right on a few points, he suggested I should try your agent. And when she'd calmed down and could speak, she said she could quite see why you'd developed cold feet. That the description of Major Cantrell was altogether too exact, and adjustments would have to be made.'

He grinned faintly. 'So the facial scars are going, and his eyes have turned an attractive blue. It seemed safer than risking the likes of Penny referring to us as Hugo and Mariana for ever and a day.'

He paused. 'Mrs Morgan also said that you were almost certainly clinging to the idea of Hugo as villain because you didn't want to admit your own feelings had changed. But once you'd come to terms with that, the whole book took off like a rocket.'

Her colour deepened. 'But it isn't for sale any more. Sonia…'

'Sonia is not an issue,' he said. 'Not if she values her job. And your book is for sale, my darling. I told Mrs Morgan that, as your future husband, I was authorising her to put it back on the market. And I bribed her for your home address with the promise that she can be godmother to our firstborn.'

There was a tap on the door and Mrs Paget entered with the coffee tray.

She looked from one to the other and her brows lifted. 'Mr Benedict, you seem to have made my daughter cry. I hope for your sake that they're happy tears.'

He said quietly, 'I intend to ensure they will be, Mrs Paget, for the rest of our lives together. And my name is Mark.'

She nodded. 'My husband has a surgery this morning, but he'll be back for lunch. Perhaps you'll stay and join us.' At the door, she turned. 'A nice hotpot, I think. Such a warm *family* meal.' And went.

When they were alone again, Tallie said shakily, 'I think the banns are safe, if you're really sure you want me.'

'I want you,' he said gently. 'And I always will. In fact I'm having a hell of a job keeping my hands off you, potential interruptions and snoring dogs notwithstanding. But more importantly, I love you, Tallie, and I need you to share my life.

'But it's your script, darling,' he added. 'This may not be an inn in Portugal, but you still have to supply the happy ending.'

He held out his arms and she went to him, the words springing to her lips as she looked up at him, smiling through the last of her tears.

'Oh, my love, my love,' she quoted softly. 'Please take me home.'

And, like Mariana, she lifted her mouth to his in trust and total surrender.

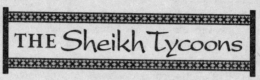

Exclusively His

Back in his bed—and he's better than ever!

Whether you shared his bed for one night—
or five years—certain men are impossible to forget!
He might be your ex, but when you're back in his bed,
the passion is not just hot, it's scorching!

Things get tricky for sensible Veronica when
she unexpectedly meets Lucien again after one
night in Paris. And now he's determined to
seduce her back into his bed....

PUBLIC SCANDAL, PRIVATE MISTRESS
by **Susan Napier**
#2777

Available in November.

*Look out for more Exclusively His novels
in Harlequin Presents in 2009!*

I ♥

HARLEQUIN® *Presents*

BROUGHT TO YOU BY FANS OF
HARLEQUIN PRESENTS.

We are its editors and authors
and biggest fans—and we'd
love to hear from YOU!

Subscribe today to our online blog at
www.iheartpresents.com

REQUEST YOUR FREE BOOKS!

2 FREE NOVELS
PLUS 2
FREE GIFTS!

YES! Please send me 2 FREE Harlequin Presents® novels and my 2 FREE gifts (gifts are worth about $10). After receiving them, if I don't wish to receive any more books, I can return the shipping statement marked "cancel". If I don't cancel, I will receive 6 brand-new novels every month and be billed just $4.05 per book in the U.S. or $4.74 per book in Canada, plus 25¢ shipping and handling per book and applicable taxes, if any*. That's a savings of close to 15% off the cover price! I understand that accepting the 2 free books and gifts places me under no obligation to buy anything. I can always return a shipment and cancel at any time. Even if I never buy another book, the two free books and gifts are mine to keep forever.

106 HDN ERRW   306 HDN ERRL

Name	(PLEASE PRINT)	
Address		Apt. #
City	State/Prov.	Zip/Postal Code

Signature (if under 18, a parent or guardian must sign)

Mail to the **Harlequin Reader Service:**
IN U.S.A.: P.O. Box 1867, Buffalo, NY 14240-1867
IN CANADA: P.O. Box 609, Fort Erie, Ontario L2A 5X3

Not valid to current subscribers of Harlequin Presents books.

Want to try two free books from another line?
Call 1-800-873-8635 or visit www.morefreebooks.com.

* Terms and prices subject to change without notice. N.Y. residents add applicable sales tax. Canadian residents will be charged applicable provincial taxes and GST. Offer not valid in Quebec. This offer is limited to one order per household. All orders subject to approval. Credit or debit balances in a customer's account(s) may be offset by any other outstanding balance owed by or to the customer. Please allow 4 to 6 weeks for delivery. Offer available while quantities last.

Your Privacy: Harlequin Books is committed to protecting your privacy. Our Privacy Policy is available online at www.eHarlequin.com or upon request from the Reader Service. From time to time we make our lists of customers available to reputable third parties who may have a product or service of interest to you. If you would prefer we not share your name and address, please check here. ☐

HP08R

HARLEQUIN *Presents*

EXTRA

MARRIED BY CHRISTMAS

For better or worse—she'll be his by Christmas!

As the festive season approaches, these darkly handsome Mediterranean men are looking forward to unwrapping their brand-new brides.... Whether they're living luxuriously in London or flying by private jet to their glamorous European villas, these arrogant, commanding tycoons need a wife...and they'll have one— by Christmas!

HIRED: THE ITALIAN'S CONVENIENT MISTRESS
by CAROL MARINELLI (Book #29)

THE SPANISH BILLIONAIRE'S CHRISTMAS BRIDE
by MAGGIE COX (Book #30)

CLAIMED FOR THE ITALIAN'S REVENGE
by NATALIE RIVERS (Book #31)

THE PRINCE'S ARRANGED BRIDE
by SUSAN STEPHENS (Book #32)

Happy holidays from Harlequin Presents!

Available in November.

HPE1108

Coming Next Month

Plus, look out for the fabulous new collection *Married by Christmas* in Harlequin Presents® EXTRA: